Has Christina pushed Sterling too far?

"Let's try this again." Christina urged the mare forward. Sterling got within a foot of the stream, then started to whirl left. Christina tapped her left side with the crop. Pulling hard on the right rein, she forced the horse back toward the stream.

Sterling froze, her whole body stiff. Christina blew out a breath of frustration. Why was Sterling being so pigheaded? She tried to remember what Mona had told her to do. *Use the crop to teach your horse to move forward when you ask. If you don't make her obey, she's only going to get worse.*

Christina reached back and smacked Sterling a little harder. Startled, Sterling leaped forward, landing in the water.

"We did it!" Christina crowed.

Suddenly, Sterling started to shake. Her head and ears drooped; her hindquarters trembled.

Christina clapped her hand over her mouth, stifling a cry. She'd thought she was such a hotshot rider, making Sterling go into the water. Now she realized the awful truth. Sterling wasn't being stubborn. She was scared to death!

And by forcing her into the stream, Christina had lost the mare's trust.

Collect all the books in the Thoroughbred series

Collect all the books in the Ashleigh series

* coming soon

THOROUGHBRED

CHRISTINA'S COURAGE

CREATED BY
JOANNA CAMPBELL

WRITTEN BY
ALICE LEONHARDT

HarperPaperbacks
A Division of HarperCollins*Publishers*

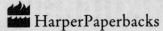**HarperPaperbacks**
A Division of HarperCollins*Publishers*
10 East 53rd Street, New York, N.Y. 10022-5299

This book contains an excerpt of Thoroughbred #28: *Camp Saddlebrook*. This excerpt has been set for this edition only and may not reflect the final content of the paperback edition.

This is a work of fiction. The characters, incidents, and dialogues are products of the author's imagination and are not to be construed as real. Any resemblance to actual events or persons, living or dead, is entirely coincidental.

ISBN 0-06-106529-3

HarperCollins®, 📖 ®, and HarperPaperbacks™ are trademarks of HarperCollins*Publishers,* Inc.

Cover art © 1998 by Daniel Weiss Associates, Inc.

First printing: June 1998

Printed in the United States of America

Visit HarperPaperbacks on the World Wide Web at
http://www.harpercollins.com

❖ 10 9 8 7 6 5

CHRISTINA'S COURAGE

CHRISTINA REESE LAY IN BED AND STARED UP AT THE FLOW-ered wallpaper, pink curtains, and white canopy bed she'd had since she was six. It all looked so babyish now. Except for two gigantic horse posters that she loved, she was ready to tear the room apart and redecorate.

Stretching, she kicked off the sheet. The sun was already streaming through the window, so Christina knew she'd slept later than usual. This summer had been so hot she'd been getting up extra early to ride her horse, Sterling Dream, in the cool morning hours. But today she felt like being lazy.

Suddenly, her bedroom door flew open with a bang. "Ta da!" Melanie Graham, Christina's cousin, stood posed in the doorway, her arms raised as if she'd finished a cheer.

1

"So, what do you think?" Melanie asked as she tipped her head from side to side. Her short, light blond hair was streaked with rainbow colors.

"You look like a cone of rainbow sherbet," Christina said. Sitting up, she swung her bare feet to the floor.

Melanie had been living at Christina's house since the beginning of the summer, and Christina still wasn't used to having someone her age around all the time, much less barging into her room. Not that she didn't like Melanie, but sometimes her crazy cousin from New York City was too much.

Melanie pouted. "That's all you have to say? I mean, it took forever. I had to clip back each section of hair so when I poured on the Kool-Aid the colors wouldn't run into each other. You ought to try it on your hair."

"No way." Christina ran her fingers through her tousled strawberry-blond mop. Bending, she searched for the jeans she'd thrown on the floor the night before. "You didn't have anything better to do, like pony horses or muck out a stall?"

"I did that already while you were *sleeping*," Melanie said pointedly. "It's after ten o'clock, you know."

"Well, I was doing important things like wondering what to do with this stupid room." Christina waved her arm. "It's too babyish."

"It is kind of juvenile." Cocking her head, Melanie

2

looked around the room. "A few posters of the Headknockers would spice the place up." Her gaze swung back to Christina, who was pulling her jeans from under the bed. "How come you're not riding this morning?"

"I've got a lesson later, and I didn't want to tire out Sterling before then. We've got a lot of work to do this summer if we're going to move from novice to training level."

Christina competed in combined training, a sport often called eventing. Beginning eventers rode in novice and training-level horse trials that usually included dressage, stadium jumping, and cross-country jumping.

"You're thinking about moving up already?" Melanie sounded surprised. "I mean, you just competed in your first horse trial."

"I know. And it proved Sterling and I are ready." Christina pulled on her jeans, then hunted around for her USCTA T-shirt.

"Just because you and Sterling won doesn't mean you're ready for the big fences."

"We didn't win it. The team did. And I've been jumping three-six all spring, so training-level fences won't seem hard at all." She finally found her T-shirt under a pile of clothes on her desk chair. On the front it had a silk-screen design of a horse jumping a huge Swedish oxer.

She grabbed it and went into the adjoining

bathroom. The *pink* bathroom, she noted as she pulled off her nightshirt. Weren't almost eighth graders too old for pink?

"I guess. And you and Sterling did have the best score," Melanie called from the other room.

"Right." Christina smiled at the memory. Despite the sloppy weather and Christina's just-healed broken wrist, she and Sterling had done a great job.

Christina slid on her T-shirt, then stared at her reflection in the mirror. Hazel eyes surrounded by thick lashes stared back at her, and her hair stuck out every which way. She looked almost as wild as Melanie.

Grabbing her brush, she yanked it through the tangled mess as if she were combing out Sterling's thick tail. Sterling Dream. Sometimes she still couldn't believe the gorgeous gray mare was hers.

Before Christina bought her, Sterling had been a racehorse. But the mare's heart hadn't been in racing—just like Christina's heart wasn't in racing, even though her parents owned one of the finest Thoroughbred breeding and training facilities in Kentucky. Christina's dream was to compete in three-day events.

Her instructor, Mona, told Christina that she would need a special mount in order to become an expert event rider. And the first time Christina saw Sterling, she knew the mare was the horse she'd been looking for. Winning the Foxwood Acres Horse Trials had proven she was right.

"It's time to train for the Olympics!" Christina announced to her reflection in the mirror as she tugged out the tangles in her hair. She had big plans. As soon as she reached the required age of fourteen, she wanted to ride in a three-day event. That meant working and training hard this summer.

"Your mom said I could go with you to Mona's for the lesson," Melanie said, appearing in the doorway of the bathroom.

Christina quit brushing her hair. "Great. Who are you going to ride?"

"Trib."

Tribulation, nicknamed Trib, was the pony Christina had ridden before buying Sterling. Since Melanie was smaller than Christina, she'd be just about the right size for the talented, feisty jumper.

"Think you can handle him?" Christina grinned at Melanie in the mirror.

"Sure. He can't be harder to handle than Pirate." Pirate was a blind racehorse that Melanie had retrained as a track pony, a horse used to accompany the racehorses to and from the training track.

"Don't underestimate Trib. He's small but mighty."

Melanie shrugged. "We'll do okay. You'll see."

"Okay-y-y." Christina wasn't as confident as Melanie. Trib had managed to dump her many times, and she'd been riding a lot longer than Melanie. "Mona's doing a group lesson today. It's not until seven this evening when it cools off, which means we need to leave here about six. We better eat an early dinner. I'll tell Mom."

Melanie snapped her fingers. "Oh, that reminds me. Your mother wants us to meet her in the mare and foal barn at eleven."

"Uh-oh. What'd we forget to do? Put a brush away? Sweep a speck of dust from the aisle?" Christina's tone was joking, but her words were true. Ashleigh Griffen and Mike Reese, her parents, were tough taskmasters when it came to running Whitebrook Farm. With three barns, a training track, a dozen employees, over fifty horses, and acres of pastures, the farm needed constant and careful supervision. And the hard work had paid off. Whitebrook was known all over the country for producing winning racehorses.

"Nah, she didn't sound angry," Melanie said. "I think it has something to do with the weanlings."

"The weanlings?" Christina turned to face Melanie with a puzzled look. A weanling was a foal that had just been separated from its mother.

"Yeah, the adorable weanlings. They're so cute!" Melanie gushed.

"They are cute." Brushing past her cousin, Christina headed back into her room. Her stomach was grumbling. "I'm going to grab something to eat before meeting her."

"I'll come with you." Melanie helped Christina make her bed, then the two went downstairs into the big country kitchen. The only sign of breakfast was the stack of rinsed dishes in the sink.

Christina knew her parents had eaten hours ago. They usually got up at dawn to begin working the horses. Even though they had a trainer and assistant trainer, Ashleigh and Mike kept close watch on their horses' training, and Ashleigh, a prize-winning jockey, still rode.

"We ate all the blueberry muffins," Melanie said, no trace of apology in her voice. She knew they were Christina's favorite. "And boy were they delicious."

"Gee, thanks." Opening the refrigerator, Christina hunted for something to quiet her rumbling stomach. Instead, she found a carrot for Sterling.

She stuck the carrot in her back pocket, then shut the refrigerator door. Melanie was leaning against the counter, a sly grin on her face. "You are too easy to con, cuz," she said. Pulling her hand from behind her back, she gave Christina a muffin wrapped in a napkin.

"Where'd this come from?"

"I saved it for you."

"Thanks," Christina said, but then she narrowed her eyes suspiciously. "Why'd you save it? Is it some kind of bribe? Do you want me to muck out Pirate's stall for a week?"

"Wel-l-l-l." Melanie drew out the word. "It is sort of a bribe. I wasn't sure how happy you'd be when I said I was going to ride Trib."

"Oh." Christina hadn't even thought about that. She'd been so caught up in working with Sterling lately, she'd pretty much neglected her pony. "Actually, I'm glad you're going to give him some attention."

"In that case, I'll take it back." Melanie grabbed for the muffin.

"No way!" Laughing, Christina whipped it out of Melanie's reach. As she dashed outside, she took a quick bite.

The morning sun was bright, and Christina wished she'd worn her cap. She went through the gate in the picket fence, then crossed the drive, finishing the muffin as she hurried toward the three red-trimmed barns on the hill. Beside her, Melanie chattered excitedly about the evening's lesson and how she wanted to work on jumping. But Christina wasn't really listening. She was thinking about Saturday's horse trial at Foxwood Acres.

Because of her wrist, she almost hadn't been able to compete. At the last minute, the other team members—Katie and Dylan, and Cassidy Smith, a new girl who was supposed to take her place—had convinced her she should be the one to ride Sterling.

Christina smiled as she remembered how nervous she'd been. But when she'd checked the standings at the end of the day, she and Sterling had had the best individual score. It had been a dream come true.

"There's your mom," Melanie said as they approached the barns.

8

Christina looked up. Ashleigh stood in front of the open double doors of the training barn, her arms crossed. She was talking to one of the grooms, but she kept glancing toward the two girls.

Christina waved. Just then, a shrill whistle rang from the training barn on the left. Kevin McLean came striding toward Christina and Melanie. Kevin was the twelve-year-old son of Ian McLean, Whitebrook's head trainer. Since the McLeans lived in a cottage on the farm, Christina and Kevin had grown up together.

"Wait up." Kevin broke into a jog. He wore jeans and a tank top. A baseball cap covered his auburn hair.

When he reached them, he stopped in his tracks and raised one hand, shielding his green eyes. "Whoa, get me my shades. This girl's hair is blinding."

"It's not that bad." Melanie put her hands on her hips in mock anger, then started laughing. "Are you meeting Ashleigh, too?"

"Yup. Hey, are you two coming to the baseball game tomorrow night?" Kevin asked as he fell into step beside them. "Dylan's pitching," he told Christina, wiggling his brows.

Everyone knew Christina had a crush on Dylan Becker, a guy her age who rode at Mona's. When they'd found out their team had won at Foxwood, Dylan had kissed Christina on the cheek.

Christina blushed just thinking about it.

"I'd love to come and watch," Melanie said. "What's your position, Kevin? Bench warmer?" she teased.

"I'm the catcher. Not a glamorous position, but—"

"—one of the most important positions on the team," Christina finished Kevin's sentence. She'd heard him say it so many times, she knew it by heart.

"Will you guys hurry up?" Ashleigh called. The groom had left, but Christina's mom was still standing in the open doorway. "I've got to leave in a few minutes to meet Mike."

"Where's Dad?" Christina asked as they walked up.

"He's gone to look at a broodmare at Oakbridge Manor." Turning, Ashleigh went into the barn, with Christina, Kevin, and Melanie right behind her.

The building was cool and dark. In the summer, the horses were kept inside during the hot, buggy hours of the day, then turned out at night. In the winter, the routine was reversed.

The mare and foal barn was Christina's favorite. She loved the babies, plus Sterling, Trib, and Jasper, Kevin's horse, were stabled at the far end along with Wonder, Ashleigh's first racehorse, who was twenty-four years old and retired.

"Hi, Shining. Good morning, Fleet." As she followed her mom down the wide aisle, Christina greeted each mare and foal. She used to know all the names of the horses on the farm, but lately she'd been so busy with Sterling that she'd lost track.

Stopping halfway down the aisle, Ashleigh turned to face the others. "Here they are," she declared, waving her arm at a trio of stall doors. "Your projects until school starts."

"Our projects?" Christina went up to a door and peered in. A fuzzy-faced weanling with a white star peered back.

"Oh, he's so adorable!" Melanie cooed as she came up beside Christina and hung over the wooden door to get a better look.

"I'd like you to work with them every day," Ashleigh said.

"Every day!" Christina cried. How would she have time to work with Sterling?

"They'll need grooming, leading, tying, clipping, and loading lessons," Ashleigh went on. "Any questions?"

"I get the grooming and leading part," Melanie said. "What do you mean about the other stuff?" Since Melanie had ridden at Clarebrook Stables in New York City, she'd been used to well-ridden and much-handled older horses.

"These babies have never been taught to stand quietly while tied, or had their whiskers or fetlocks trimmed with clippers," Ashleigh explained. "And if you practice loading them in the van and trailer now, they'll be used to doing it by the time they're yearlings."

"Oh." Melanie still looked confused.

Ashleigh laughed. "Don't worry. There are several

11

books in the barn office about training foals. Plus, Kevin and Christina have both worked with youngsters. Follow their leads."

"I'll help you all you want, Mel." Kevin gave her a big smile.

"Great." Reaching over the stall door, Melanie scratched the foal's forehead.

Ashleigh checked her watch. "I've got to go."

"Wait, *I* have a question," Christina said. "How am I going to have time to get Sterling ready for our next competition, do my other chores, *and* work with a weanling?"

"It's summer, so you have all day," Ashleigh replied. "Besides, Sterling's still young and green. She's only been off the track for a month. I noticed you rode her Sunday and Monday right after the competition. You might want to give her a break."

Christina rolled her eyes. She hated it when her mother gave her advice. "I only rode on the trail. Besides, I want to do several training-level competitions before summer's over. That means—"

"That means you'll find a way to fit in your work on the farm with your big plans," Ashleigh said. Putting her arm around Christina's shoulder, she gave her a hug. "I know you, Chris. You'll find a way. And working with the weanlings is important. Last year's crop didn't get enough attention. By the time they were yearlings, they were tough to handle. I don't want that happening again."

"Me either," Kevin said. "Once they're yearlings, they're strong enough to drag you anywhere they want," he told Melanie.

Ashleigh gave Christina one last squeeze. "I've got to run. You guys pick which weanling you want, then let me know. Okay?"

"Okay!" Melanie exclaimed enthusiastically.

Christina folded her arms in front of her. It wasn't okay with her, but she knew there was no way she would change her mother's mind. Lots of people envied her because she'd grown up on a horse farm. But sometimes it seemed like her parents' passion for racehorses came before whatever Christina wanted.

Only *this* time, Christina decided as she watched her mother leave, she was going to make sure *nothing* got in the way of her eventing dream. Absolutely nothing.

13

2

A NICKER FROM A STALL AT THE END OF THE AISLE CAUGHT Christina's attention. *Sterling!*

Forgetting about the weanlings, she hurried to the end of the barn. Sterling's head hung over the Dutch door. Her ears were pricked, her neck arched as she whiffled a greeting.

"Hey, girl." Christina ran her palm down the mare's face, her heart catching in her throat. Every time she saw Sterling, she was amazed at the mare's grace and beauty. And not only was she gorgeous, she could jump like a deer.

"Don't worry, I didn't forget you." Christina pulled the carrot from her pocket. "I might have to work with a foal, but I'll still find time for your training. 'Cause we've got big dreams, right?"

"Which foal do you want, Chris?" Kevin called down the aisle.

15

"Don't care," Christina called back as Sterling took the carrot daintily between her lips and crunched it noisily. "Be back in a minute," she told the mare. Sterling bobbed her head, her big eyes wide, her expression eager. Christina gave her one last pat before heading down the aisle.

Kevin was opening a stall door. "Melanie picked Terry. I'm taking Rascal. You get Missy."

"Is Terry short for Terrible?" Christina teased Melanie.

Melanie was still leaning over the stall door, scratching the star on her weanling's forehead. The bay foal wiggled her lips in delight. "If it is, then this sweetie pie was misnamed."

"And how about Rascal?" Christina said to Kevin as she looked in the stall. "Is that any indication how much trouble Fleet's latest colt is going to give you?"

"I don't think he's going to give me any trouble." Kevin was standing beside the jet black foal whose head came up to his shoulder. He held the halter with one hand while he ran the other hand down the weanling's knobby front legs.

Christina watched him for a second. Kevin had a gentle touch, just like his dad. "It still sounds like I got the best of the three," she told him. "With a name like Missy, she's bound to be an angel."

"You never know. Missy's out of Miss Respectable, that new mare your dad bought last year. She was

16

already in foal to some stallion standing in Maryland, so we don't know what her baby's going to be like."

"Well, she'd better be an angel since I'm not going to have much time to work with her." Christina went next door to Missy's stall. The chestnut filly was fine boned with a small dished face. Her fuzzy mane stood straight up and her short tail flipped back and forth. When she saw Christina, she pricked her ears curiously.

"O-o-o, you are beautiful," Christina crooned as she unlatched the door. Except for the color, the filly reminded her of what Sterling might have looked like when she was young. Maybe working with Missy would be fun after all.

But when she swung open the door and stepped into the stall, Missy wheeled around. With a squeal, she kicked out her hind legs.

Startled, Christina jumped back just in time. Missy crow-hopped into the corner, then turned and pinned her ears. Christina's mouth fell open. She'd never seen a foal act so defiantly.

Behind her, Kevin whistled. "Whew. I think maybe you better ask your mom for another baby. That one's going to be tough."

Christina shook her head. "No. I can handle her. She just needs time. She needs to know I'm her friend."

"And she needs to know who's boss," Kevin added.

17

"That too." Christina shut the door behind her. She hoped she was right about the foal needing time. Otherwise, Missy would soon be a nickname for "Big *Mistake*."

Christina ran the body brush down Sterling's belly, making her dappled coat shine like a new dime. It was six in the evening, and the mares and foals had been turned out. The barn was blissfully, peacefully quiet.

"Ouch!" Melanie's cry of anguish broke the silence. "He bit me!"

Covering her mouth, Christina squelched a giggle. Pint-sized Trib was up to his old tricks.

"Tighten the girth slowly," Christina called across to her. "And don't forget to check it before you mount."

Dropping the brush in the grooming box, she opened the stall door. She had to hurry and tack up Sterling before the lesson.

She reentered the stall with the bridle draped over her shoulder and the saddle and pad cradled in her arms. Sterling was standing with her nose in the corner, her hind end toward the door.

"Not you, too," Christina moaned. Sterling was usually eager to be ridden. She couldn't still be tired from Saturday's event. That had been four days ago. Maybe she should have given Sterling a few days off after the competition.

Melanie led Trib from his stall. The brown-and-white pony hadn't been ridden since Christina had brought Sterling to the farm. His mane had grown out and his belly bulged.

Christina laughed. "No wonder he bit you. He's so fat, his girth probably doesn't fit anymore."

"It fits," Melanie said. "But it's several notches lower." She patted Trib's neck, then put on her riding helmet. She was wearing her purple-fringed lavender-colored chaps. "Gee, it's too bad I have to wear this helmet. My hair matches my chaps."

Christina glanced down at her own brown chaps. They were boring in comparison. "I'll be ready in a minute," she said as she went into Sterling's stall. Immediately, the mare swung her head around and eyed Christina warily.

"What is wrong with you?" Christina asked. She put the pad on Sterling's back, then lifted up the saddle. When she set it down on top of the pad, the mare switched her tail. Christina straightened the pad, then tightened the girth. After taking off Sterling's halter, she walked around to the left side to bridle her. The mare stuck her nose in the air.

"Hey!" Christina lowered the bridle. Sterling had never done that before. What was going on with her? Reaching up, she cupped her fingers around Sterling's nose and pulled down her head. This time, Sterling didn't resist. Quickly, Christina put the bridle on, smoothing the mare's forelock under the brow band.

When Sterling was a racehorse, her groom had abused her. Every time she was around him, she'd acted half crazy. But in the time she'd been at Whitebrook, Sterling had grown to trust Christina.

I hope nothing's happened to change her behavior, Christina thought.

"Hurry up!" Melanie hollered. "We'll be late."

"We'll take the shortcut by the road," Christina said as she opened the door and led Sterling from the stall. Melanie was already walking Trib down the aisle.

Halting Sterling, Christina checked her over to make sure nothing was wrong with the saddle or bridle. As Trib left the barn, Sterling nickered for her stablemate.

"Feeling better?" Christina asked. The mare bobbed her head as if to say yes.

When Christina got outside, she shoved her helmet on and snapped the strap. Melanie was standing on the mounting block, but every time she tried to put her foot in the stirrup Trib sidestepped away.

"He won't stand still," Melanie complained.

"Here." Christina grabbed the cheekpiece of Trib's bridle. "Now get on."

Melanie sprang into the saddle. Instantly, it tipped sideways. "Uh-oh. I forgot to tighten the girth."

"I'll do it," Christina offered.

Melanie shifted her weight to get the saddle

balanced again, then swung her leg back. Lifting the flap, Christina pulled the girth up an inch.

"I'm not doing too great, am I?" Melanie said gloomily. "I mean, you'd think I was a beginner."

Christina smiled. "It is the first time you've ridden Trib. He's sneaky. You're used to Pirate. Thoroughbreds are big and powerful, but ponies are quick and crafty. You have to be one jump ahead of them."

"I should understand that. It's the same thing my dad says about being a parent to me." Melanie sighed. Her father, Will Graham, was a record producer in New York City. He didn't have much time to spend with Melanie, and during the last school year Melanie had gotten in some trouble. That was one reason she was spending the summer at Whitebrook.

Picking up her reins, Melanie rode Trib away from the mounting block so that Christina could get on. Sterling stood quietly as Christina swung her leg over the saddle, but before Christina could get her feet in the stirrups the mare moved off.

"Whoa." Christina made her halt before giving her the signal to follow Trib. The pony was striding eagerly across the stable yard. Since most of the other horses had been fed and turned out or put up for the evening, the place was quiet.

"I think he's ready to go!" Melanie called over her shoulder.

Christina agreed. "He's been bored since I got Sterling. You'll be good for him."

She hoped she was right. Melanie was pretty impulsive. Before she left New York, she'd done some stupid things with horses, and since she'd been at Whitebrook she'd only ridden Pirate. The one time she'd ridden Sterling, Melanie had ignored Christina's instructions and the mare had run away with her. But Christina figured that if her mother had given Melanie permission to ride Trib, she must have confidence that Melanie had become more responsible.

"I'm glad Mom suggested you ride him," Christina said.

When Melanie didn't answer, Christina grew instantly suspicious. *Had* Melanie asked permission?

"Mel?" Christina urged Sterling into a trot. Trib was jogging down the edge of the drive toward the main road. But Sterling had such a long stride, she quickly caught up to him. "You did ask Mom, didn't you?"

"Uh." Melanie shot her a guilty grin. "Well, sort of."

"What do you mean 'sort of'?"

"I sort of said that *you* said it was okay. Then she sort of said it was okay."

"Melanie!" Christina sat deep in the saddle and pulled Sterling to a halt at the end of the drive. Beside her, Trib planted his feet and stopped dead. Melanie lurched forward, catching herself on the pommel.

"Ouch." She grinned sheepishly at Christina. "Looks like maybe this was a mistake, huh?"

"Maybe. Only you're going to have to go through with it now. Even if you get dumped."

"Dumped?" Melanie repeated in a small voice.

"Yeah." Christina thought back to the time Melanie had pulled a fast one on her when her family had visited New York City. They'd gone to Clarebrook Stables to rent horses for a ride in Central Park. Melanie had made sure Christina had gotten the worst mount at the stables. Spooked by a dog, the horse had bolted. Christina had managed to stick tightly.

Maybe it would serve Melanie right if Christina pulled a fast one on her. If she and Sterling took off down the grassy roadside, Trib would break into a gallop to catch up. And usually when Trib galloped, he bucked.

"I just wanted to take a lesson," Melanie explained. "Not only do I want to be a better rider, but all your friends keep their horses at Mona's. I'd like to get to know them better."

"Then why didn't you just tell that to Mom instead of sneaking around?"

Melanie shrugged. "I guess I'm just used to conning grown-ups."

"You conned me, too," Christina pointed out.

"Sorry."

Melanie sounded so sincere, Christina relented. "All right. Let's get to the lesson. At a walk. We've got time, and I *guess* I don't want Trib to dump you."

23

"Good," Melanie said with undisguised relief.

Christina turned Sterling onto the wide shoulder of the main road. The sun was sinking lower, so it wasn't quite so hot, and part of the roadside was shaded. When several cars flew past, Sterling flicked her ears nervously, but Christina soothed her with a pat on the neck. The mare's stride was so long, Trib had to break into a jog to keep up.

"Mona's doesn't seem this far when you drive in the car," Melanie said.

"It's only a mile and a half from Whitebrook," Christina told her. "Look. There's the sign at the end of the fence line: Gardener Farm."

Melanie glanced nervously over her shoulder. "The cars go really fast on this road."

"Trib's used to it."

"Still—" Melanie licked her lips nervously. Christina suddenly realized why her cousin was so worried. Milky Way, the horse Melanie had ridden in New York City, had fallen in the road and been killed by a taxi cab. It had been a horrible accident and partly Melanie's fault. Christina knew Melanie would never forget it.

"Chris," Melanie said in a low voice. "Slow down. Trib's starting to get jiggly."

Twisting around, Christina glanced over her shoulder. The two had fallen about twenty feet behind. Trib was tossing his head and prancing sideways.

24

"Loosen your reins and let him catch up," she said. "I don't want to be late. If I'm going to move out of novice competitions, every lesson counts."

"Okay." Melanie didn't sound too confident. Trib broke into a trot, his short legs pumping. Christina was about to turn back around when she heard the roar of a motor and a tractor trailer came thundering around the turn behind them. As it sped toward them, the driver blasted the air horn.

Sterling jumped ten feet in the air, throwing Christina off balance. Then the mare spun into Trib. To avoid crashing into her, the pony scooted onto the road. The air horn blasted again and Trib scrambled to get out of the truck's way.

Christina heard Melanie scream. Tightening her hold on Sterling, she got the mare under control just in time to see Trib slip on the asphalt. His metal shoes skidded on the slick pavement, and he fell to his knees in the middle of the road.

This time, Christina screamed.

3

"MELANIE, GET OUT OF THE ROAD!" CHRISTINA CRIED.

Melanie had fallen forward onto Trib's neck, dropping the reins. Quickly, she straightened and gave Trib a swift kick.

"Go," she shouted, her voice frantic. Reaching down, she grabbed the dangling rein. Trib scrambled to his feet as the truck bore down upon them.

At the last second, it swerved onto the shoulder, rumbling and bumping in the grass. Trib leaped to the side as the truck cut back onto the road and roared away without slowing down.

When it had disappeared around the bend and Christina could no longer hear the sound of the motor, she let her shoulders sag with relief. "You two could have been squashed like bugs!"

"Really. Roadkill," Melanie tried to joke, but her

face was as white as a sheet. Christina jumped off Sterling. Trib's neck was soaked with sweat, but when she ran her hands down his front legs there wasn't even a scrape.

Melanie dismounted. Her legs buckled and she had to hold onto Christina. "That was a close one." She gave Trib a hug. "If it hadn't been for Trib, we would have been history. You did great, buddy."

"You did great, too, Mel. I was afraid you were going to panic and lose it. But you pulled it together and got Trib to safety."

Melanie smiled weakly. "I did do okay, didn't I? And for once it wasn't me who almost caused a disaster. I couldn't have handled another horrible . . ." She didn't finish her sentence, but Christina knew what she was talking about. "I mean, I was being supercautious when that crazy truck blasted his horn." Anger flared in Melanie's brown eyes. "He never even slowed down! Do you think he didn't see us?"

"I don't know. I'm just glad no one was hurt."

For a second, the four just stood there. It was so quiet and the road was so empty—it was hard to believe that a minute ago a truck had almost run them over.

"I think I'll *walk* to the Gardeners' drive from here," Melanie finally said.

"Me too. My legs feel like rubber. It'll give the horses a chance to calm down, and I want to see if Trib hurt himself."

Turning, Christina pulled the reins over Sterling's

head. When she started to lead the mare forward, Sterling rolled her eyes toward the road, then skittered sideways.

Trib strode off with no sign of soreness. When they reached the drive, the two girls mounted. "Do you think we should tell anyone?" Melanie asked.

"No. You know grown-ups. They'd never let us ride along the road again. Not that I want to for a couple of days." Christina shuddered. "I just hope it's not going to make the horses scared of trucks."

"Naw." Melanie slapped Trib affectionately on the neck. "This guy's forgotten about it already."

Christina wasn't so sure about Sterling. As they walked up the drive, the mare spooked at every rustling leaf and dark shadow.

Not a good way to start a lesson, Christina thought. Maybe she should skip it today. But then she remembered that Mona was expecting friends this weekend. They were staying at the Gardeners, which meant Mona might not be able to squeeze in another lesson. And Christina couldn't afford to miss a lesson. She and Sterling had too much to work on.

"There's Dylan." Melanie waved. Up ahead, Dylan was trotting his horse, Dakota, around Mona's big outdoor ring.

If Christina's face hadn't already been so red, she would have blushed at the sight of him. Not only did she think he was unbelievably cute, but he looked great on a horse.

"Now don't you think you better go to that baseball game tomorrow night?" Melanie teased.

"Well, maybe. Yeah, probably," Christina agreed, and the two girls started laughing.

Then Christina saw her best friend, Katie Garrity, trot her horse, Seabreeze, into the ring. Christina stopped laughing. Mona had started the lesson without them!

"Great," Christina muttered. "We're late."

"We did have a good reason," Melanie said.

"Only we're not telling anybody the reason, remember?"

"Right. Then what should we tell them? I'm great on making up stories about why I broke my curfew or skipped school, but I don't know any late-for-lesson lies."

As they approached the gate into the ring, Mona turned to look at them. The instructor was the same age as Christina's mom, and she had a muscular build from years of riding. Mona wore shorts and sunglasses and carried a bottle of water.

Christina chewed her lip, trying to think of a good reason why they were late. "I'll say Sterling got a rock in her hoof," she whispered to Melanie.

"Good plan."

Mona walked over to the gate. "You girls are late. Is everything okay?"

"Sterling had rocks in her head," Melanie blurted.

Christina shot her cousin a keep-your-mouth-shut

30

look. "She meant Sterling had a rock in her hoof," she corrected.

Mona was looking curiously at them. "Are you sure you're all right? Trib looks a little lathered for such a short trip."

"It's hot." Christina fanned herself with her hand to demonstrate her point. "And he's out of shape."

"That's for sure." Mona eyed the pony. "It's good you're going to ride him, Melanie. He needs to lose a few pounds." She opened the gate and stepped back to let them through. "We're just warming up, so you didn't miss anything."

"Good." Christina urged Sterling into the ring, eager to get away from Mona. She hated lying to her instructor, but there was no way she wanted to tell her about the close call. Mona would tell Christina's parents, and they would overreact and not let Christina ride to her lessons. And if she had to rely on someone at the farm hauling her in the trailer, she might never get a lesson the rest of the summer.

As Dylan rode by, he gave her a megawatt smile. His brown eyes were shadowed by the brim of his helmet, but still Christina could feel his gaze on her. Instantly, her insides turned to mush. She'd definitely go with Melanie to tomorrow night's baseball game.

Christina sighed dreamily, totally forgetting she was in a riding ring on a horse until Sterling snorted and broke into a jog, jolting her forward.

"Chris, are you with us this evening?" Mona called.

Flushing with embarrassment, Christina nodded. She had to get her mind off boys and onto the lesson.

"Just work your horses at a relaxed working trot," Mona instructed. "You want them balanced and light."

Holding the reins softly, Christina squeezed her calves against Sterling's sides. The mare moved right off into a trot, but her neck felt stiff, and when Trib charged past she put her ears back.

"This isn't a race, Melanie," Mona called. "I know this is your first time on Trib, but you need to remind yourself that you're the driver. Post a little slower, sit a little deeper. If he doesn't respond, trot him in a tight circle."

Melanie turned Trib right in front of Katie and Seabreeze. Breeze was part quarter horse and part Thoroughbred, so she was smaller and stockier than Sterling. She was also calmer, though she hated any horse coming too close.

"Okay, everybody in the center of the ring for a minute." Mona raised her voice to be heard over the clopping of the horses' hooves.

Christina asked Sterling to walk. Dylan steered Dakota, an Appendix registered quarter horse, beside her, and together they went over to where Mona was standing. Dakota stretched his neck to sniff at

Sterling. He was a big-boned, handsome chestnut, but Sterling wanted nothing to do with him. Pinning her ears, she gave him an ugly look.

"I've decided that in two weeks we're going to have a schooling dressage show here at the stable. At the Foxwood Horse Trial, your cross-country scores were much better than your dressage scores, so we need to work on the test movements."

Christina slumped in the saddle. Mona couldn't possibly be talking about her. After all, she and Sterling had won.

"Fortunately, your horses jumped well despite the lousy weather. Still, the fences were small. We've got to work on getting your horses supple and balanced so they can handle larger, trickier jumps."

"More jumping sounds great to me," Christina agreed.

"Only we're not going to do more jumping," Mona said. "We're going to concentrate on dressage. Can anyone tell Christina why?"

"Dressage teaches your horse to be obedient, supple, and balanced," Katie said as though she were reading from a textbook.

"That's right. So we're going to work on dressage for the next two weeks. Then we'll have our schooling show."

"But I don't get it," Christina protested. "Dressage is trotting and cantering around in a bunch of circles. How's that going to help us with our jumping?"

"Dressage teaches you to communicate with your horse and turn him into a better athlete," Dylan said.

"It's kind of like ballet," Katie added. "You and your horse need to be graceful, but powerful and controlled, too."

Christina stared at them with a look of horror. What was with these two? Were they serious? She didn't like dressage nearly as much as jumping. It was boring and repetitive, not fast and exciting. Besides, Sterling had trouble over water jumps, often refusing or ducking out. Even though they'd made it over the ditch at Foxwood, Christina knew they had to school over lots of fences before they could handle the trickier water jumps.

"The dressage show will just be for my students," Mona continued. "I'm having Frieda Bruder judge it. She'll go over each of your scores, explaining what you need to work on."

"But I know what I need to work on," Christina said. "Liverpools, banks, oxers. Otherwise, Sterling's never going to make it around a training-level course."

"Slow down, Christina," Mona said. "Don't rush Sterling. She needs lots of work learning to use herself. She still wants to stick her nose out and run like a racehorse. One day that's going to get you in trouble over fences."

Christina opened her mouth to protest again, but Mona was already telling the others more about the schooling competition. Gloomily, she stared down at Sterling's withers. Mona sounded just like her mother.

I shouldn't be surprised, Christina thought. *Mona is Mom's best friend.*

What she couldn't understand was why everybody kept telling her not to rush Sterling. Couldn't they see what a natural jumper she was?

Reaching down, Christina scratched the mare's neck. She knew Sterling better than her mother or Mona did. She knew the mare better than *anyone.* She knew what Sterling needed in order to be an event horse. And that was lots of jumping.

Forty-five minutes later, when the lesson was over, Christina and Melanie rode home the long way through the woods. The sun was setting, and they knew they had to hurry.

"Boy, that was the most boring lesson I've ever had," Christina grumbled as they went up the hill behind Mona's barn.

"Well, I was kind of hoping to jump, too," Melanie said. "But you know, after all the sitting trot and collecting stuff, Trib was more responsive."

Christina chuckled. "You mean he was bored to death."

"No. He was lighter. And I felt lighter." Melanie cocked her head. "Does that make sense?"

Christina burst out laughing. "Maybe you both lost ten pounds."

"Ooh, don't make me laugh." Melanie grabbed her ribs. "I've got a side ache from all that bouncing in the saddle."

"Only you're not supposed to be bouncing." Christina made her voice sound like Mona's. "You're supposed to be moving with the horse."

"Yeah, maybe if you're Dylan," Melanie said. "He and Dakota looked great."

Christina gave her cousin a sharp look. "You're not getting a crush on Dylan, are you?"

"No way. I like the rugged, casual type—someone with a sense of humor."

Christina choked back a giggle. "Not *Kevin*."

Blushing, Melanie glanced sideways at her. "Well, he is sort of cute."

"Kevin?" Christina repeated. She'd known him for so long that she couldn't even imagine thinking he was cute.

Melanie pointed her finger at her. "Yes, and don't you dare say anything to him!"

"I won't. I've got other things to worry about. If we're not going to jump at Mona's for the next two weeks, I'll have to school Sterling over bigger fences on my own."

"Isn't that risky?" Melanie asked, riding ahead. They'd entered the woods and Trib led the way down the path.

"I'll be careful. In fact, a good place to start would be the cross-country trail Kevin and I made."

"Well, count me out. I'll do what the rest of the group does."

"Okay," Christina replied, but her thoughts were already on jumping. She had wanted to work over water today, and it just dawned on her how she could do it before going home.

"Mel, up ahead there's a fork. Take the path to the right."

"To the right? But that doesn't go home. And it's starting to get dark."

"It goes down to the stream. We can let the horses have a quick drink." *And I can get Sterling to go over it,* Christina thought.

"I'll lead." Christina steered Sterling off the path and around the pony. Branches whipped her in the face. A deerfly settled on the mare's neck, drawing blood before Christina could swat it.

The path grew steeper as it descended toward the stream. Christina balanced her weight. Behind her, she could hear Trib crashing through the underbrush.

When they reached the edge of the stream, Christina let Sterling lower her head. The mare stood about two feet away and snorted at the gurgling water but wouldn't get any closer.

Trib stomped right into the water, stirring up mud. He slurped noisily, then started to paw.

"Watch he doesn't roll," Christina cautioned. She looked across the stream. There was no bank on the other side, the footing looked solid, and the path

37

going up the hill wasn't steep. It would be a perfect place to cross.

"I'm going to try and get Sterling over the stream," she told Melanie. "Ride Trib to the other side and stand about halfway up the hill. Sterling will want to join him."

"Now?" Melanie protested. "But I'm tired and—"

"Oh, come on, Melanie. I've *got* to get Sterling used to water. She jumped the ditch at Foxwood with no problem, so it should only take a minute."

"All right." Turning Trib around, Melanie rode him from the stream. When they'd gone halfway up the hill, Sterling nickered anxiously.

"Perfect. I bet she follows him." Christina shortened up on the reins, then nudged her with her heels. Sterling took one step forward, panicked, and ran two steps back, knocking into a tree trunk. She leaped sideways into some brambles.

"Come on. It's just a little stream. Nothing scary," Christina said while she bumped the mare's side with her boot heels.

Sterling took one baby step down the path, then snorted and tried to spin to the left. Christina checked her with an outside rein and leg.

"Let's try tomorrow," Melanie called, sounding tired.

"No!" Christina gritted her teeth. Sterling was really being stubborn. But Christina could be just as stubborn. "We're not going home until she goes over the water."

Melanie sighed. Reaching overhead, Christina pulled a skinny branch from the tree. She couldn't let the mare get away with it now, or she'd never get her in the water. She'd have to win this battle—and quick. At the horse trials, when Sterling had tried to refuse, a little tap behind the saddle had done the trick.

"Now let's try this again." She squeezed the mare with her legs, urging her forward. Sterling got within a foot of the stream, then started to whirl left again. Christina tapped her left side with the branch. Then, pulling hard on the right rein, she forced the horse back toward the stream.

Sterling froze a foot away from it, her whole body stiff. Christina blew out a breath of frustration. Why was Sterling being so pigheaded?

The mare had balked over water many times, but Christina thought she was over it. Her mind whirled, trying to remember what Mona had told her to do. *Use the crop to teach your horse to move forward when you ask. If you don't make her obey, she's only going to get worse.*

Holding the reins in one hand, Christina reached back and smacked Sterling a little harder. Startled, Sterling leaped forward, landing in the water. Christina flew into the air, losing her stirrup before thumping back into the saddle. When she righted herself, Sterling was in the middle of the stream.

"We did it!" Christina crowed.

"Good. Let's go home," Melanie said.

"I'm ready." Christina sighed with relief. She'd won the battle.

Suddenly, Sterling started to shake. "Hey, it's all right." She ruffled the mare's mane, but Sterling didn't respond. Her head and ears drooped; her hindquarters trembled.

Christina clapped her hand over her mouth, stifling a cry. She thought she was such a hotshot rider, making Sterling go into the water. Now she realized she hadn't won any battle at all. Sterling wasn't being stubborn. She was scared to death!

And by forcing her into the stream, Christina had lost the mare's trust.

4

"ARE YOU READY TO GO?" MELANIE ASKED AS TRIB PICKED his way down the path to the stream.

Christina looked up at her cousin, tears in her eyes. Quickly she wiped them away. She didn't want Melanie to know that she'd blown it, that she never should have forced Sterling into the stream.

Because Sterling had been abused by her groom back on the track, Christina had never wanted to use a crop on her. Mona had practically insisted, and in a way Christina knew her instructor was right. But it would have been better to listen to her own instincts.

Melanie halted Trib at the water's edge. "What's wrong? Is Sterling hurt?"

"No. She's just tired," Christina fibbed.

"Me too." Trib sloshed into the stream, then stretched out his nose to snuffle Sterling.

Picking up the rein, Christina turned Sterling around. The mare burst from the water as if she were afraid it was going to burn her. When they made their way up the hill, Christina threw the switch as hard as she could into the woods.

She wasn't any better than the groom that had whipped Sterling at the racetrack. When Christina had brought her mare to the farm, she had worked hard to create a bond between them. And now she'd ruined it!

How could she have been so stupid?

"We want a pitcher, not a glass of water!" Melanie cheered from the bleachers. Sitting next to her, her chin propped on her palms, Christina stared miserably across the baseball diamond. Kevin and Dylan's team was at bat, but she wasn't paying much attention.

"Strike three," the umpire said.

Melanie jumped to her feet. "Strike three! That was a mile wide!"

"Melanie." Christina glanced up at her cousin. "Quit hollering—you're embarrassing me."

Giving her a huffy look, Melanie plopped beside her on the metal seat. Her rainbow-striped hair was spiked with mousse, and she wore purple sunglasses, a bright blue T-shirt, and orange shorts. Christina was almost blinded by the combination.

"Well, *you're* embarrassing me," Melanie retorted.

"The Blue Jays are losing by two runs and you won't even cheer them on."

"They're losing?" Christina frowned in confusion. "I thought they were winning."

"That was before that giant of a guy on the Rockets hit a grand slam. Weren't you paying attention?"

Christina shrugged. "I guess not." She sighed. Ever since yesterday, she couldn't get her mind off Sterling. Once a horse had a bad fright, it took forever to get over it. Would Sterling ever be confident over water?

And more importantly, would she ever trust Christina again?

Reaching over, Melanie felt Christina's forehead. "I think you're coming down with something. Your head's hot. Your face is flushed. Must be L-O-V-E." Giggling, Melanie gestured toward the dugout. "Dylan's up next."

Christina turned her attention to home plate. She *was* sorry the Blue Jays were losing. Dylan, Kevin, and many of her other classmates had practiced and played hard all summer. Still, she couldn't concentrate on the game when all she could think about was how badly her plans were falling apart.

Since spring, all she'd thought about was eventing. She'd gotten her perfect horse and even won her first horse trial. Now it seemed as if everything were going wrong. Sterling hated water. Mona didn't want her to jump. And Christina herself had made the biggest mistake of all—forcing her horse to do something it didn't want to do.

This morning, she hadn't ridden at all. When she brought Sterling in from the pasture, she spent half an hour just grooming her. Sterling had almost sighed with relief.

But Christina wanted desperately to compete in at least a few training-level horse trials before summer was over. She and Sterling had to be fit and ready to tackle a variety of jumps. But the way things were going, they'd never make it. And she had no idea what to do about it.

Melanie elbowed her in the side. "Dylan's up!"

Shading her eyes from the setting sun, Christina focused on Dylan. His uniform was covered with dust, and his cheeks were smeared with dirt. Still, he looked really cute, and she was glad Cassidy Smith hadn't come to the game to watch. She thought Cassidy might have a crush on Dylan, too.

"Did I miss anything?" Beth McLean, Kevin's mom, slid into the bleachers beside Christina. "I dismissed my aerobics class early so I wouldn't miss the last inning."

"They're losing by two runs," Melanie said, peering around Christina. "Now Dylan's up, Jacob's on first, and there are two outs."

"Strike one!" the ump called.

Melanie leaped up. "Strike one! That almost bounced on the plate!"

"Get a pair of glasses, ump!" Kevin's mom yelled.

As the Rockets' pitcher got ready to throw, the crowd grew silent. Christina held her breath. The ball whizzed into home. Whack! Dylan hit a grounder past the shortstop.

"Yes!" Christina punched her fist in the air as Dylan raced to second base while Jacob ran to third.

"Two men on and Kevin's up!" Beth said breathless with excitement. "Has he been hitting well?"

"Uhhh." Christina and Melanie looked at each other. Neither wanted to say anything.

Beth groaned. "That bad, huh?"

"His catching has been great," Melanie said. "And he made a super double play. Only he struck out twice. The Rockets' pitcher is really good."

"Well, let's hope he does better this time. They need this hit."

"Come on, Kevin!" Melanie screeched. "Hit it out of the park!"

Throwing them a big grin, Kevin stepped up to home plate. The pitcher eyed him, then let the ball fly.

Crack! It arced high and long. Everybody on the bleachers jumped to their feet. As the ball soared over the center fielder's head, Dylan and Jacob raced for home.

Melanie grabbed Christina's shoulders. "It's gonna be a home run!" she yelled as she bounced up and down.

45

"Go, Kevin! Go!" Beth screamed on the other side of Christina.

When Kevin pounded into home, sliding to miss being tagged, the whole team rushed from the dugout. They'd won by a run.

"Whew." Beth slumped on the bleachers.

Christina sat down beside her. "I bet you're glad you didn't miss that!"

Kevin's mom grinned. "That's for sure. I just wish Ian had been here."

"Why wasn't he? He usually doesn't miss a game."

"He went with your dad to pick up that new broodmare he bought yesterday," Beth explained. "Is your mom here?"

Christina shook her head. "No. She dropped us off and went to get groceries. Dylan's mom is taking us home."

Beth stood up. "I'll see if Kevin wants a ride home."

"Oh, I think he's going with Dylan, too," Melanie said quickly.

Arching one brow, Beth stared at Melanie, then her face broke into a big grin. "Okay. Tell him congratulations for me. He's surrounded by such a crowd, I won't get a chance."

"We will." Christina said good-bye, then turned to Melanie. Her cousin had jumped off the bleachers and was heading over to the dugout where several

46

guys were pouring water containers over Kevin's head.

Christina thought about following her but decided against it. Instead she went over to the concession stand and ordered a soda.

Growing up in New York, Melanie had a confidence that Christina definitely lacked. Sometimes, Christina wished she were more like her cousin.

After paying for the drink, Christina went over to a picnic table behind the backstop and sat on the top. Gesturing dramatically, Melanie stood by the dugout talking to Kevin and a couple of other kids Christina recognized from school. Christina couldn't help but wonder what her cousin was saying that had them so captivated.

"Hey. What'd you think of the game?" Dylan asked, walking up behind her.

"It was exciting," Christina said. "Your last hit was great." She held up her soda can. "Thirsty?"

"No, thanks." He grinned and Christina's heart melted. His face was so dirty it made his teeth look whiter and his brown eyes brighter than ever.

"I think I drank a gallon of water already," he said, sitting down next to Christina.

Suddenly feeling tongue-tied, Christina took a quick sip of her soda. When she and Dylan were at Mona's, they had no trouble talking. But here on the baseball field, she felt awkward.

"Doesn't your arm get sore after pitching so many innings?" she asked.

"Yeah. Real sore." He rotated his shoulder. "Sometimes when I groom Dakota, it feels like it's going to fall off."

"Don't mention falling off," Christina said, and they both laughed. At Foxwood, Dylan had fallen off Dakota into a mud puddle, and earlier Christina had broken her wrist getting dumped during a lesson.

Tipping back his cap, Dylan glanced sideways at her. "So what did you think about yesterday's lesson?"

"It was okay."

"I really like dressage."

"I'd much rather jump." Christina dropped her gaze to her feet. For a second, she twirled the soda can in her hands. She thought about telling Dylan what was bugging her but quickly decided against it. He rarely made a mistake in his riding, and she made so many.

A piercing whistle made her look up. Kevin and Melanie were in the parking lot standing by a green Jeep.

"My mom must be ready to go," Dylan said.

"Right." Christina slid off the picnic table.

As they walked to the parking lot, Christina glanced over at him at the same instant he looked at her. She burst into nervous giggles. "It seems funny not to be riding side by side with you."

48

"Yeah. But I like it. I think we should do it more often."

Christina's eyes widened and she slowed. What exactly did he mean? But Dylan had walked ahead, and she couldn't see the expression on his face.

"Would you two hurry up," Kevin grumbled good-naturedly. He'd taken off his cap. Not only was he dirty, but his hair and shirt were soaked with water. "Your mom's making me run behind the car."

Dylan eyed him. "I don't blame her. You're really grungy."

Christina greeted Mrs. Becker when she reached the car. Dylan's mother was as gorgeous as her son was handsome. She wore tailored outfits that fit her slender figure perfectly, and her shoulder-length brown hair was styled in a sleek bob.

"Get the beach towel out of the trunk," Mrs. Becker told Dylan. "Kevin can put it on the front seat."

Melanie was already in the back. Christina bet she was mad she wouldn't get to sit next to Kevin, but that meant Christina would get to sit next to Dylan.

Quickly, she climbed in and Dylan slid in beside her. As they drove home, they all discussed the game.

"That umpire couldn't tell a strike from a ball," Melanie finally said. Sitting forward, she leaned on the back of the front seat.

"That's for sure," Kevin agreed, and the two launched into a heated discussion about the officiating.

"You okay?" Dylan asked in a low voice.

Without looking at him, Christina nodded. She couldn't look at him. He was so close, she'd probably blush five different shades of red. "I'm fine."

"You're pretty quiet. Something on your mind?" He snapped his fingers. "Wait. Let me guess. You're thinking about riding."

Christina smiled. "Right. I guess I do have a one-track mind."

"Anything bugging you?"

He sounded so sincerely interested, Christina decided to tell him. Maybe he could help her figure out what to do. "It's Sterling. And me. And being frustrated because we're not clicking."

"I thought you were doing great, considering she's just off the track."

Tilting forward, Christina turned her body slightly toward him. "Only she should be doing greater. She's got such ability and she loves to jump. There's no reason why we shouldn't be doing training level."

"Except that neither of you are ready."

"What do you mean?"

"You and Sterling aren't a team yet," Dylan said. "I've been riding Dakota for three years, and we still have lots to work on. Sterling's green, and there's so much to learn about eventing. I mean, winning one horse trial doesn't mean you're ready to move up a level."

Christina shot him an angry look. Dylan sounded

just like Melanie, her mother, and Mona. Why were they all against her?

She slumped back in the seat. Mrs. Becker was turning down Whitebrook's long, winding drive. *Hurry up and get me home,* Christina thought.

"If it makes you feel better, I don't think any of us are ready for training level. Except maybe Cassidy."

Cassidy. Christina frowned. Why was he bringing up her name? Cassidy *was* an experienced and talented rider, but that didn't make her an expert eventer.

"Thanks for the vote of confidence," Christina said in a low voice just as Mrs. Becker pulled up in front of the house.

Melanie opened the car door. Christina quickly thanked Mrs. Becker, and pushing past Melanie, jumped from the car.

Without waiting, she raced up the steps and into the house. Slamming the door behind her, she leaned against it.

So much for a romantic ride home, she thought sourly. If Dylan couldn't understand how important her dreams were, there was no way she could like him. From now on, she would keep her problems and plans to herself.

5

"THE GAME WAS PRETTY COOL, WASN'T IT?" MELANIE SAID later when she came into Christina's bedroom. "So what were you and Dylan talking about the whole way home?"

Christina had already showered and was in bed reading her *Practical Horseman* magazine, hoping to discover something about balky horses and water. "Dylan who?" she asked without looking up.

"Oooooh." Melanie plopped down on the edge of the mattress, making the bed bounce. "I thought I noticed a bit of anger as you plowed past me, stormed up to the house, and slammed the door in my face."

She said it so dramatically, Christina couldn't help but laugh. "Was it that obvious?"

"Unless you were Kevin." Pretending to swoon,

Melanie fell back on the bed, right on top of Christina's legs. "He didn't notice. All he could talk about was the game."

Christina laughed again. She couldn't believe city-girl Melanie was acting so goofy about country-boy Kevin. To her, he would always be the kid next door.

"So are you going to tell me what you and Dylan talked about?" Melanie asked as she propped herself up on one elbow.

"No." Throwing the magazine to the floor, Christina pulled the sheet to her chin. "So go away."

"Not until you tell."

"Aren't you tired?"

"No." Melanie bugged her eyes out. "I can stay up all night."

Christina believed her. Melanie had pulled some wild stunts in New York, sometimes sneaking out after her dad was in bed.

"We were talking about horses."

"Horses?" Melanie gave her a funny look. "That's romantic."

"I wasn't trying to be romantic. There are other things to think about besides boys."

"True." Melanie chewed her lip as if thinking. "Though right now I can't name any."

Groaning loudly, Christina pulled the sheet over her face. "Go away!"

"So why were you talking about horses?" Melanie asked.

Christina didn't say anything. She heard Melanie sigh, then the mattress jiggled and the springs squeaked as if her cousin had taken the hint and left. But when Christina pulled the sheet off her face, Melanie was standing next to the bed, grinning. "Fooled ya."

"You are really annoying." Christina made a face at her.

"Yeah, I am. So are you going to tell me?"

"No."

This time Melanie got the hint. Shrugging, she turned and headed out the door. "Okay, be that way. But don't expect me to confide any of *my* secrets to you," she added as she waltzed out the door with a hurt expression.

"You don't have any secrets," Christina hollered after her. "You tell everybody everything that's on your mind."

"Not true!" Melanie hollered back. Then a door shut and the hall was silent.

Christina held her breath, waiting for Melanie to come charging back, and was almost disappointed when she didn't. Melanie could be irritating and nosy, but she was also funny. Christina needed all the laughs she could get right now.

When Christina woke up Friday morning, she knew what she needed to do with Sterling. She needed to take the mare down to the stream and let her get used to the water—even if it took all day.

After dressing quickly in old breeches and a T-shirt, Christina made her bed, brushed her hair, and grabbed several carrots. Then she pulled on her waterproof riding boots instead of her leather paddock boots. She'd probably be needing them since convincing Sterling to go in water might mean wading in herself.

It was early, and the stable area teemed with activity. Anna Simms, one of the farm's exercise riders, was riding a long-legged two-year-old toward the training track behind the barns. Christina waved. Anna raised her whip in a return hello, then the colt spooked at something, and the two jogged away. Christina glanced toward the training barn, wondering if Melanie was helping pony horses this morning. She didn't see her cousin, but Kevin was walking a sweaty horse with a blue-and-white cooler draped over its back. Christina recognized the pretty filly. It was Leap of Faith, a three-year-old who was having a successful racing season.

When Kevin saw Christina, he waved her over.

"I'll talk to you later!" Christina called. She didn't want to get sidetracked. The older Kevin got, the more involved he was with the racehorses. He probably wanted to talk about Faith's great workout or Shining Moment's wind puffs. And Christina didn't want to hear it. Right now, all she wanted to think about was Sterling.

Kevin caught up with her, anyway. "Why are you in such a rush?"

"I want to ride Sterling before it gets hot." Christina paused long enough to stroke Faith's silky neck. Her father had bought the filly at an auction a few years ago. She'd been gangly, thin, and awkward. Mike had taken the chance that she'd grow into something special, and Faith had proved him right.

"Why don't you let Sterling have the day off?" Kevin asked.

"She had a day off yesterday. Besides, what do you know about training event horses?"

"Nothing, but I know horses. And your mare's starting to look as worn out as a racehorse after a hard season."

"Gee thanks," Christina said dryly. If one more person tried to tell her how to take care of Sterling, she was going to burst!

When she entered the mare and foal barn, she could hear the sounds of feed buckets thunking and teeth chomping. Around six A.M., the stable help brought the horses in from outside and fed them. Since Sterling was out on pasture all night, she didn't get much hay. By now, she'd be through her grain and ready for an easy workout.

"Christina, look!" Melanie called. She was walking down the aisle, leading her weanling. "Terry is doing great."

"That's super," Christina said as she ducked into the tack room to get her grooming box.

With a firm *whoa*, Melanie halted Terry outside the door. "How's Missy doing?"

"Missy?" Christina felt a stab of panic. She hadn't even thought about Missy since the day her mom had assigned them the job of working with the weanlings. "Oh, she's okay. I haven't had much time to work with her. I should be able to this afternoon," she added as she came out of the tack room.

"Are you riding?"

"Yeah. I'd invite you to come along, but Sterling and I are going down to the stream."

"You're not getting in another fight with her, are you?"

Christina shook her head. "Absolutely not. This time I'm using bribery."

Melanie laughed. Growing impatient, Terry stamped her little hoof, then tried to nip Melanie on the arm. "All right, I'll get moving. We'll walk over to the training barn and see the two-year-olds, and I'll tell you all about becoming a racehorse."

Melanie waved good-bye, and Christina went in to brush Sterling. When she opened the stall door, the mare pricked her ears and whinnied, happy to see her.

"Thank goodness you're not mad at me today," Christina said as she snapped the lead onto the halter. She gave her a brisk brushing, then tacked her up, putting the bridle on over the halter. Coiling up the lead line, she attached it to the saddle. She'd need it once they got to the stream.

"Now a little fly spray." Christina gave Sterling a spritz before they left. This time of the year the deerflies would be thick in the woods.

By the time Christina led Sterling outside, most of the racehorses had already finished their workouts and the stable area was full of Thoroughbreds being bathed, walked, and hosed down. A horse in training might only be ridden for fifteen to twenty minutes, but the care to keep them sound, healthy, and fit required hours.

Christina spotted her mom. Ashleigh was bent over, running her hand down the front leg of a two-year-old colt named First Term who was out of Terminator, one of Whitebrook's stallions. All Thoroughbreds' birthdays were officially January first no matter when they were born. First Term had been born in June, so he was still a young "two-year-old." His training had to go slow and easy until his tendons and muscles were strong enough to withstand the strain of running.

When Ashleigh straightened, she saw Christina and waved. Christina mounted Sterling, then rode over to say good morning to her. Instantly, First Term arched his neck and pranced on the end of the lead, eager to impress Sterling. Fortunately, his groom, Mark Anderson, was used to handling young horses who were full of themselves. Using firm words, he settled First Term before leading him off.

"Is Term okay?" Christina asked.

Ashleigh nodded. "Just keeping an eye on him. He's so bullheaded he thinks he should be galloping around the track instead of trotting."

"Bullheaded like his sire," Christina said. Whenever she visited the stallion barn, she gave Terminator a wide berth.

"Where are you off to?" Ashleigh asked.

"Just a trail ride."

"That sounds nice." Ashleigh sighed. Christina thought her mother looked tired. She was so caught up in the day-to-day running of the farm that she never had time to ride for pleasure anymore.

"Why don't you come with me one morning?" Christina asked.

"I'd love to, but when would I find the time?" Ashleigh waved her arm to encompass the farm. "Taking in outside horses for training has helped finances, but it's been a lot of work."

Christina nodded, though her mind was already escaping to the woods. Her mom and dad lived and breathed racehorses. Galloping around a track at breakneck speed was not Christina's idea of fun, and after a while she tuned out racing talk.

"How's Missy?" Ashleigh asked.

"Missy?" Christina repeated, immediately turning red. "U-uh," she stammered, not sure what to say.

"I'm really anxious to see how she works out," Ashleigh went on as if she didn't notice Christina's hesitation. "She's out of Chesapeake, that hotshot stallion from Maryland. If Missy turns out okay, we might breed another mare to him."

Christina gulped. Fibbing to Melanie was one thing, but she knew from experience that lying to her mom would only backfire later. "I haven't had time to work with her yet."

Her mother frowned. "Chris, I expect you—"

Her mother's tone of voice and the fact that Christina already felt guilty immediately put her on the defensive.

"Why can't you see it my way for once?" she cut in before her mother had a chance to finish. "Missy may be important to you, but she's not to me. Mona's having a schooling show, and Sterling and I need to be ready."

Ashleigh's eyes narrowed. "Christina Reese, if I was asking you to spend all day working on the farm, I would expect protests. But I have only asked you to work with one weanling. Melanie and Kevin are managing to fit it in."

"Melanie and Kevin don't want to become an Olympic event rider," Christina argued right back.

"I know that's your dream," Ashleigh responded. "But that's way in the future, which means that right now you need to do your chores." She pointed at Sterling. "And you have to stop pushing this horse.

You know what happens to racehorses when they're pushed too hard. They break down or quit. That's going to happen to Sterling if you keep acting like she's ready for the Olympics."

Christina gritted her teeth. "Sterling isn't just *any* horse, Mom. And I think I know what's best for her. Besides, you don't care about my eventing. You want me to be interested in every foal, stallion, and mare on this place, but *you* never even take the time to find out what I like. So don't lecture me about what I want to do!"

With those angry words, Christina turned Sterling and set off across the stable yard at a trot. She didn't dare look back at her mother. She and Ashleigh had butted heads before, but this was the worst fight they'd had in a long time.

As Christina trotted up the hill toward the woods, leaving Whitebrook behind, tears filled her eyes. Why had she gotten so mad at her mother? Deep down, she knew Kevin, Dylan, Mona, and her mom were only trying to help. So why was their advice rubbing her the wrong way?

She'd been especially unfair to her mother. Her jab about Ashleigh not supporting her hadn't been true. Her mother was the one who had bought Sterling, trusting Christina's judgment when everybody else had said the mare was too crazy for a kid to handle. And even if Ashleigh hadn't been to every show or horse trial, Christina knew she was always rooting for her.

It must be me. When she woke up that morning, Christina felt as if she had a handle on things. But now she knew she was wrong. She was falling apart and she knew why—she was losing confidence in her ability to work with Sterling.

When had that confidence disappeared? she wondered.

The answer wasn't hard to figure out. Her confidence was lost back when Sterling had refused a jump, causing Christina to fall off and break her wrist. That day, a tiny seed of fear had been planted. She'd thought winning the horse trial had gotten her over her fear. But she was wrong.

At the top of the hill, Sterling settled into a relaxed walk. Christina took a deep breath, trying to take the kink out of her neck and the knot from between her shoulder blades. But they wouldn't go away. What if she couldn't get Sterling to go over water—*ever?*

That won't happen! Christina told herself firmly. But no matter how firmly she said it, she wasn't totally sure it was true.

She was sure of one thing: When she got back from the ride, she'd have to apologize to her mother, no matter how hard it was to say, "I'm sorry."

After riding in the hot sun, the woods felt deliciously cool. Christina avoided the cross-country trail that she and Kevin had built out of downed logs and branches. It seemed so long ago that she and Trib had galloped pell-mell over the makeshift jumps without a care.

She steered Sterling down the path to the stream. Instantly, the mare's ears began to flick nervously. Halfway down the hill, the stream came into view, and she stopped dead.

Christina dismounted. "This is as close as you're going to get, huh?"

She ran up her stirrups. Uncoiling the lead line, she hooked it to the halter. Then she took off Sterling's bridle and laid it over a tree branch. Clucking to Sterling, she started down the path. Two feet from the stream, the mare stopped and eyed the running water suspiciously.

"That's okay." Christina fed her a piece of carrot. "From now on, any step you take closer to the water, I'll give you a bite of carrot. How's that?"

Sterling bobbed her head as if she thought it were a great idea, but when Christina walked toward the water the mare backed up. Letting out the rope, Christina waded into the stream.

"See?" she said as she swished each boot in the water. "It won't hurt."

Sterling only shook her head. Christina held out the carrot. Sterling ignored it. Christina splashed around in the water. Sterling rolled her eyes. Christina clucked, coaxed, and encouraged. Planting her hooves, Sterling wouldn't budge.

For an hour, Christina tried to get the mare to put

just one foot into the stream. Finally, after being bitten by deerflies, whacked by branches, and scratched by briars, Christina gave up.

Sterling clearly wasn't going in the water today.

6

CHRISTINA STARED INTO MISSY'S STALL. THE WEANLING stared back. Her fuzzy ears stood straight up; her brown eyes were as round and bright as marbles. She was adorable, but all Christina could think about was how she'd failed with Sterling.

"You ready for your first lesson?" Christina asked the little foal. Only she wasn't so little, Christina realized. Terry's head only came up to Melanie's shoulder. Missy was almost as tall as Christina.

Maybe I shouldn't tackle this right now, Christina thought. She was feeling pretty low. Handling a spunky six-month-old took plenty of skill, concentration, and determination. Right now, she had zero of all three. But then she remembered how mad her mother had been, and she knew she couldn't put it off any longer. Besides, Melanie hadn't had any problems with her weanling. Why should she?

Remembering how the foal whirled around the first time she'd gone in the stall, Christina had saved one chunk of carrot. Opening the stall door, she held it in her hand. The foal was about to bolt into the corner when curiosity got the better of her. She stretched out her head to sniff Christina's palm, and before she had a chance to take off, Christina snapped the lead line to the halter.

"Good girl!" Christina fed her the carrot. The foal crunched it daintily, then, deciding she didn't like it, raised her lip and tossed her head, throwing bits of carrot everywhere.

Christina laughed at the silly face she was making. Moving slowly, she scratched Missy's neck and withers. The foal stood rigidly but didn't try to pull free.

So far so good. Holding the cheekpiece of the halter with her left hand, Christina ran her right hand over the baby's back and rump. Immediately, Missy squealed and kicked.

"Ticklish, huh?" She'd need lots of "sacking out," an old-fashioned term coined by the cowboys. In the old days, a wrangler would take a saddle blanket and whack it all over his horse. Now the term meant that the horse needed to get used to being rubbed and touched with lots of different things.

Without letting go, Christina moved around Missy's head to the other side. Then she repeated the scratching. Again, when she ran her hand down Missy's flank, the foal pinned her ears and kicked.

If an older horse kicked while being groomed, the horse would be quickly disciplined. Kicking was too dangerous to both humans and other horses to go unpunished. This time when Christina ran her hand down the foal's flank and she kicked, Christina slapped her flank.

Startled and scared, the foal jumped sideways.

"Easy," Christina crooned, but when she tried to get close Missy scrambled away from her. Christina blew out a breath. This wasn't working at all.

Unhooking the lead line, she left Missy huddled in the corner. She shut the stall door, then threw the lead on the floor, disgusted with herself.

Nothing was going right.

Discouraged, she headed back to the house. Kevin was throwing balls to Melanie in the front yard.

"Pop up!" he hollered as he tossed one straight in the air. Mitt held high, Melanie tipped her head back and zigzagged across the lawn. She was laughing so hard, the ball hit her glove and plopped out.

For a second, Christina felt a pang of jealousy. She used to be the one to practice with Kevin. Now it seemed as if Kevin and Melanie were always together.

Scooping up the ball, Kevin threw it to Christina underhand. She caught it, though it stung her fingers.

"And number sixty-two, Christina Reese, the new first baseman, strikes out with the pitcher, Dylan Becker!" he said, talking into his fist as if he were an announcer with a microphone.

"Hey." Winding up, she threw it back to him as hard as she could. He caught it easily. "That's none of your business."

"It is if the pitcher calls the catcher and asks what's going on," Kevin said.

"Dylan called you?" Melanie asked, and when Kevin nodded, she grinned excitedly.

Christina put her hands on her hips. "When? And why and what did he say?" she demanded.

Kevin wiggled his brows. "Now she wants to know."

"Kevin McLean, if you don't tell me, I might have to mention to Melanie the time you asked B—"

With a horrified look, Kevin rushed over and clamped his mitt over her mouth. "Don't say it," he warned.

Melanie rushed over, too. "What? What were you going to say about Kevin?"

Kevin gave Christina a murderous look. She pushed away his hand. "Don't worry. I won't tell. As long as you tell me what Dylan said."

"He just wondered why you stormed out of the car last night," Kevin said offhandedly as he tossed the ball in the air.

"As if you know the answer," Melanie huffed. "You were too busy doing instant replay of the game."

"Hey, I know exactly why Christina was mad. I told him you were really worried about Sterling and that any criticism of the way you were handling the precious princess sent you into orbit."

"It does not," Christina protested.

"I told him you'd get over it. That you were so anxious to be an eventing star, you'd gone a little wacky."

"Not true!" Christina snapped. Kevin's comments made her mad, especially since part of her realized he was right. "I'm just tired of everybody telling me how to ride my horse!"

She must have yelled because Kevin and Melanie stopped what they were doing and looked at her strangely. Spinning around, Christina stormed across the yard to the house. She was tired of horses, tired of everybody's advice, tired of messing up.

It was time to redecorate her room.

Half an hour later, Christina was standing on her desk chair, sliding her pink ruffly curtains off the rod, when she saw her mother come up the sidewalk. She glanced at the clock on her bedside table. It was after twelve. Her mother was coming in for lunch. Maybe this would be a good time to talk to her.

She jumped off the chair. Dropping the rod on the bed, she hurried down the stairs and into the kitchen. Ashleigh stood in front of the open refrigerator door.

She looked up when Christina came in. "Hi. Does tuna fish sound okay?"

Christina nodded. "I'll be happy to make a salad. Are Dad and Melanie coming for lunch?"

"Dad is. Melanie went with Kevin and his mom to the hardware store. They were going to stop and get burgers somewhere."

"That's nice." Christina busied herself getting salad bowls from the cupboard. Suddenly, she wasn't sure what she wanted to say. Setting the bowls on the counter, she turned to her mother. "Mom, I—"

"Chris, I—" her mother started at the same time.

They laughed. "You go first," Christina said.

"Okay." Shutting the refrigerator door, Ashleigh set the mayonnaise and lettuce on the table. "I'm sorry for criticizing you. I'm really proud of you. You've worked hard with Sterling. She's come a long way."

"Thanks." Christina ducked her chin.

"Now what did *you* want to say to me?" Ashleigh prompted as if she knew she were owed an apology, too.

"I'm sorry I got mad at you. You have been supportive, and I do need to do my chores."

Ashleigh gave her daughter a quick hug, then started opening the cans of tuna fish. "Now that we got that over with, what's the real problem?"

Christina glanced up sharply. "There's no problem," she said quickly. Too quickly, she realized when she saw her mother's dubious expression.

"I know something's up," Ashleigh said as she took off the lid and drained the oil.

Grabbing the lettuce, Christina started to make the

salad. "Do you think Dad will want cucumbers?" she asked, trying to change the subject.

"Yes. Carrots, too. Though there don't seem to be any left. Have you been feeding them to Sterling again?"

"Uh-huh." Christina ripped up hunks of lettuce, then sliced the cucumber. After a few minutes, she looked up. Her mother had stopped working and was watching her.

"I know you're worried about something," she said. "Does it have to do with Sterling?"

Christina shook her head. She wasn't ready to tell her mom everything. She didn't want another lecture. Besides, Sterling was her problem and she needed to figure out what to do on her own.

"No, it's Missy," she said, which was true. "She's a little witch."

Ashleigh chuckled. "I thought she might be. Mark's complained about how hard she is to catch in the paddock. She won't come up unless the other two foals have gone in. Then she fights him when he leads her into the barn."

"She also kicks."

"Umm. That's not good, nor is it unusual."

"Any suggestions?"

"Oh, you want my advice?" Ashleigh said, her tone teasing.

Christina wrinkled her nose. "Yes."

"Okay. Take one of the long whips, stand by her

head, and run the end over her legs. That way, if she kicks, she's not going to get you. Do that until she's so used to being touched that she won't kick. Then you can start using your hand. It might take a long time."

"Don't hit her?"

Her mother shook her head. "No. She's too young. You'll frighten her." Ashleigh pointed a piece of celery at her. "Remember, it's essential that you combine what she doesn't like with what she likes. Scratch her head, neck, withers, and give her *lots* of attention."

Only if it doesn't interfere with my time with Sterling, Christina wanted to say, but she kept her mouth shut. Ashleigh watched her for a minute as if she knew something else were bothering her. But then Christina's dad came in and started talking about the new broodmare, and she knew she was off the hook.

On Monday evening, Melanie and Christina rode over to Mona's for a lesson. This time they took the long way through the woods. Christina didn't even go near the stream. She'd spent the whole weekend avoiding it, instead riding Sterling on a leisurely trail ride with Kevin and Melanie.

Sunday, she'd given Sterling the day off and worked with Missy. Her mother's suggestions had helped. Using the whip, she was able to keep clear of

Missy's flying back hooves. The foal still didn't like being handled, but at least Christina hadn't gotten kicked.

"I hope Mona set up a small course of fences," Christina said to Melanie as they came out of the woods. Sterling may have liked the slow weekend pace, but Christina was itching to jump.

"Oh, I can't wait to do dressage," Melanie said with exaggerated enthusiasm. "All that bouncing at the sitting trot is such fun."

But when they rode down the hill toward Gardener Farm, Christina noticed right away that the jumps had been loaded on a wagon and pulled to the far end. Even worse, Mona had staked out a rectangular arena inside the ring. All around the rectangle, she'd placed cardboard squares with bold black letters written on them.

Christina groaned at the sight. "Dressage."

"That's what the rectangular thing is for?" Melanie asked.

"Yes. I think I'll turn around and go home."

"You're joking, right?" Melanie halted Trib.

"Yes, I'm joking." Christina sighed. She wouldn't miss a lesson for anything. And she knew Mona was right. Dressage was important. She just wished they could work on jumping, too.

When they reached Mona's barn, Katie Garrity was leading Seabreeze out the big double doors. "Hi! Did you guys see what we fixed up?"

Christina couldn't believe her friend was so excited about a stupid rectangle.

"Mona, Dylan, and I worked on it all morning," Katie continued as she put her helmet on over her ash blond hair. "It was tough to get it the right dimensions because we had to use meters instead of yards, but we did it, and it's a perfect twenty-meter-by-sixty-meter standard dressage arena."

"That's great," Christina said, trying to sound excited.

"Yeah, it's really cool!" Melanie added, sounding almost as happy as Katie. "Now someone needs to tell me what you do in it."

Katie laughed, then launched into an explanation of dressage tests and why you needed the letters. She mounted Seabreeze, chattering away the whole time. And her lecture didn't slow as she and Breeze walked with Melanie and Trib into the ring.

Christina sighed. Was she the only one who'd rather jump?

Sterling shook her head, her mane flying. Christina patted her. "That's right. You'd rather jump, too."

At least I think Sterling would rather jump, Christina thought. It had been so long since they jumped, maybe they'd both forgotten how to do it.

"Hey, Chris." Dylan came out of the barn already mounted on Dakota. His greeting sounded so cheery, she wondered if he'd forgotten all about her little tantrum in his mother's car.

76

"Hi, Dylan. I see Mona's all ready for some serious dressage."

Dylan nodded. "How about you?" He eyed her with a curious expression.

Christina shrugged. "I'm going to try to get into it. I mean, I understand that it's important because it goes toward your overall score at a horse trial or event."

"Well, that's not the only reason it's—" Dylan started to say, but then he got a funny look on his face and stopped. "Never mind."

"What?" Christina prodded.

"Nope. I know what it feels like when people constantly give you advice."

"You do?"

"Yeah. I get it all the time in baseball. Being the pitcher can be a royal pain. If you're doing well, everybody loves you. If you pitch a lousy game, everybody hates you and has a hundred suggestions on what you should have done."

"Wow." Christina had no idea that perfect Dylan ever felt anything except totally confident.

"Morning, Chris," Mona greeted her as she came out of the office. Cassidy was with her. Cassidy had recently moved from Florida to Kentucky, and her horses hadn't arrived from Florida yet. Still, Christina was surprised she wasn't riding Foster, Mona's old event horse. But Cassidy was wearing shorts and sneakers, so she obviously wasn't joining in the lesson.

"Are you guys ready for a fun workout?" Mona asked.

"Sure." Christina noticed that Mona had a booklet in her head. Cocking her head, she was able to read the words "Dressage Rules" printed on the cover. Somehow, it sounded anything but fun.

"Good. Cassidy's going to help me teach."

Christina's mouth dropped open. *Cassidy? Teach?*

"Cool," Dylan said. He was smiling at Cassidy, who, Christina noted grumpily, looked as poised and cute as a model in *Seventeen*. Her blond hair was pulled back in a bouncy, shiny ponytail, and her long legs were tan and slim.

Cassidy returned Dylan's smile, then held up a piece of paper. "I've got a sample training test, so I'll yell things like 'serpentine at C' or whatever."

When they entered the ring, Mona had them warm up by trotting around the outside, staying clear of the staked-out arena.

"The arena will only be used for tests, not schooling," Mona explained. "When you leave today, I will hand out the novice-level test sheet so you can learn it for next Saturday's competition."

Novice! Christina fumed. *Why aren't we doing a training-level test?* Mona was treating them like babies.

Frowning to herself, Christina trotted past Katie. Her friend was grinning happily, obviously unfazed by the thought of riding a simple novice test where all you had to do was walk, trot, and canter.

After they went several times around the ring and Christina was about to die of boredom, Mona called, "All right, now that you've warmed up, let's sit a little deeper and ask your horses to collect."

Christina tightened her fingers around the reins and slowed her posting. Rooting her head in protest, Sterling tried to pull the reins looser. Christina gripped tighter, then sat in the saddle and tried a half halt to get Sterling to slow down. The mare stuck her nose in the air and trotted faster.

Christina sneaked a glance at Mona and Cassidy, who stood in the center of the ring. They were both watching her.

"For Thursday's lesson be ready to ride the novice test," Mona continued. "The thing I will be focusing on is your horse's way of moving. Is he accepting the bit? Is he tense? Is he resisting?"

"What do you mean by resisting?" Melanie called across the ring. Trib was speeding past everybody in his usual fast pony pace.

"The best way to explain resistance is to give you an example. Watch Sterling. She is resisting Christina. Her head has popped up, her back is hollow, and she's chewing the bit as if it was her worst enemy."

Christina flushed bright red. *Why was Mona singling out Sterling?*

"Christina is *also* resisting," Mona continued. "Instead of staying soft and relaxed in the saddle, she's making matters worse by gripping the reins, clamping her legs around Sterling's sides, and sitting stiffly. A judge would—"

The blood roaring in Christina's ears drowned out the rest of Mona's words. She couldn't believe Mona was cutting her down in front of her friends.

Tears filled Christina's eyes. She was so embarrassed, she wanted to trot Sterling out of the ring and never come back.

7

"CHRISTINA, I WANT TO SEE YOU IN THE OFFICE," MONA said after the lesson.

Christina was riding Sterling out the gate. Even though they'd been walking around the ring for the last ten minutes cooling off, the mare's neck was still dark with sweat. Under her helmet, Christina's hair and brow were soaked, too. She'd stuck out the lesson, but it had been torture, and there was no way she wanted to talk to her instructor.

"You can put Sterling in one of the empty stalls for a few minutes," Mona added, and before Christina had a chance to say, "I really can't," Mona strode away.

"Boy, she was kind of rough on you," Melanie said as she steered Trib out the gate and halted next to Sterling. "Not that she went easy on anybody else."

Standing in the stirrups, she rubbed her butt. "I may never sit again."

"At least she didn't say you were a stiff rider," Christina grumbled.

"True. But remember, later she also said that you were such a natural rider and she had confidence that you would soon quit resisting and help your horse become relaxed and supple." Melanie grinned. "Hey, I'm starting to sound like I know what I'm talking about!"

Christina dismounted and pulled off her helmet. She was so hot, her head felt as if it were going to melt. But when Dylan walked out of the ring, leading Dakota, she quickly plopped it back on. There was nothing more disgusting than flat, sweaty helmet hair.

"Are you okay?" he asked.

"Sure!" Christina said brightly. "Why wouldn't I be?"

He studied her curiously. "Because Mona was kind of tough on you."

Christina shrugged. "I can take it."

"Good lesson!" Katie came up beaming. She'd already untacked Breeze. In one hand she held a bucket with a scraper and sponge, ready to wash her horse. "I love dressage. But Mona sure was picking on you, Christina," she added in a concerned voice.

"Would everybody quit saying that," Christina exclaimed. "Mona was right. I *was* stiff and Sterling *was* resisting, but that's because we don't like dressage!"

Narrowing her eyes, Christina shot her friends a don't-say-another-word look, then led Sterling into the barn. Quickly, she ran up her stirrups and loosened the girth. She glanced at the open barn doors, hoping no one had followed her in. But when she saw that no one had, she immediately got worried. Were they all outside talking about her?

"Tough lesson, huh," someone asked behind her.

Startled, Christina whipped around. Cassidy was standing by Sterling's head, stroking the mare's face.

"No, just hot," Christina blurted.

"Really. This afternoon it was ninety-eight degrees." Cassidy ruffled Sterling's mane. "How's my pretty girl?"

When Christina broke her wrist, Cassidy had helped exercise Sterling. The two had gotten along really well. Not that Christina was surprised. Cassidy owned two horses and had competed in A-rated shows in both hunter and jumper.

"Any idea when your horses are arriving?" Christina asked before Cassidy could say anything else about the lesson. The last thing she needed was Cassidy giving her advice, too.

"Yeah. Tomorrow. I can't wait."

"That's great."

"Well, my mom's picking me up, so I better head outside. I sure enjoyed riding your horse last week,"

Cassidy said before heading down the aisle. "Maybe I can do it again sometime."

In your dreams, Christina murmured, though she knew she had no reason to be mad at Cassidy. Even though they'd had problems, Cassidy had turned into a friend. Okay, so Christina was just a teeny bit jealous, especially when Dylan was around. But who wouldn't be? Cassidy was just about perfect. Still, Christina knew she was just grumpy about everything and definitely not looking forward to talking to Mona.

From outside the barn, the sound of kids talking grew louder. Christina hurried Sterling down the aisle and into an empty stall. She didn't want to face her friends again. It was just too embarrassing. After her horrible lesson, they all must think she was the worst rider in the world.

When she took off Sterling's bridle, the mare instantly scratched her face on Christina's shoulder. "I know you're hot and itchy. When we get home, I'll give you a warm bath and a rubdown. How's that sound?"

"Great!"

Christina spun around. Melanie was grinning at her through the wire-mesh stall door.

"What do you want?" Christina asked.

"I want to know if I should wait for you or ride home alone."

Turning away, Christina shrugged. "Suit yourself."

Melanie was so silent, Christina twisted around to see if she'd gone. But her cousin was still there, staring at her, her mouth pulled down in a frown.

"You know, you don't have to act so mean to us. We are your friends," she said, then disappeared from the doorway.

Melanie's words stung. Christina wasn't being fair to anyone. Especially not to Sterling. Maybe if her mare had a sensitive, patient rider, she wouldn't be having such a hard time.

Patting Sterling, Christina left the stall and went into the office to face Mona. The instructor was sitting at her desk going through some papers. The office walls were decorated with photos, ribbons, and trophies. Mona and her students had won shows and competitions all over the state.

When Christina came in, Mona motioned for her to sit in a chair in front of the desk. Mona's fat cat, Chubby, was already sprawled on the seat, so Christina perched on the edge. Reaching behind her, she nervously scratched Chubby.

"So how'd you think the lesson went?" Mona asked without looking up.

"U-uh—" Christina stammered. She was almost ready to blurt out another cheery "great," when Mona glanced up, a serious expression on her face. Choking down the "great," Christina mumbled, "Terrible, I guess."

"Well, I'm glad we agree on one thing. I thought it was terrible, too. What do you think was the matter?"

Christina shrugged. "I'd rather be jumping."

"Why?"

"Well, dressage isn't that interesting," Christina burst out. "You do the same thing over and over, and I don't understand why we're riding a novice-level test. It's too easy."

"True."

Encouraged by Mona's agreeing with her, Christina went on: "Since I want to event, Sterling and I need to concentrate on jumping. Look at the Olympic event riders, you don't see them spending their time trotting circles."

"You don't?" Mona arched one brow.

"No! And even if they have a lousy dressage score, they can make it up over fences. I read about them all the time in my magazines: Karen and David O'Conner, Kerry Millikin, Bruce Davidson." Christina's eyes brightened. "I loved the photos of them leaping over these huge solid obstacles at the Atlanta Games. One of the jumps even had a covered bridge!"

"So you think they bought a horse and went right over those huge jumps?" Mona asked.

"Well, no. I'm sure it takes a while."

"How about ten years?"

"Ten years!"

"Well, let's look at Jill Henneberg. When she was fourteen, she bought a gray Thoroughbred mare off the track. Sound familiar? She didn't ride Nirvana in the Olympics until eight years later, *and* she ended up withdrawing because of a fall at fence thirteen."

"Eight years?" Christina repeated weakly.

"Yes, and she was unusually young. David and Karen O'Conner and Bruce Davidson have been competing forever."

"Oh." Christina fidgeted in her seat. Behind her, Chubby stretched, digging his claws into her hip.

Mona handed her a magazine. "Here's an article about Jill. You can borrow it and return it when you're done. She reminds me of you."

Gingerly, Christina took the magazine. A girl jumping a gray horse into water was on the cover. "I hope that's a compliment."

"It is." Mona smiled. "She's talented, hardworking, determined, *and* in a hurry. You know, sometimes winning your first competition isn't so hot."

"I know what you mean. I thought winning meant everything after Foxwood would be easy." With a sigh, Christina slumped back in the chair. Chubby howled a protest. "Oh!" She shot forward. "Sorry, Chub."

"Do you know why dressage is so important?" Mona asked. Sitting back, she made a steeple with her fingers.

Christina shook her head, then changed her mind and nodded. "Because it makes your horse obedient, supple, relaxed, etc., etc.," she recited in a flat voice.

"Correct. Sterling has a tendency to jump flat.

Dressage will help her use her whole body. It also teaches communication between horse and rider. Do you think that's important?"

Christina immediately thought about the past couple of days. She and Sterling were definitely not communicating, and it had made things horrible. "Yes."

"Harmony with your horse—that's what riding is all about—any kind of riding. But that's only one reason."

"What's the other reason?"

"Because it will make you and Sterling better athletes, and as you know a jumper must be a superathlete. So don't think of dressage as endless circles and half halts. Think of it as gymnastic exercises that have been perfected for centuries to develop strength, flexibility, and obedience in the horse, as well as the rider."

"Wow," Christina breathed, mesmerized by Mona's explanation. Mona made it sound as if dressage were the most important thing in the world.

Mona laughed. "Feel better?"

Christina's excitement faded. "Yes and no." She looked down at her clasped hands. "There's another problem. Even though Sterling did fine with the water jump at Foxwood, she still hates water. I can't even get her near it, and I don't know what to do."

There. She'd said it.

"Do you blame her?" Mona asked. "Most horses don't like water, and Sterling's ongoing problems with the liverpool didn't help. Even at the horse trial, you had to hit her to get her over the ditch."

Then I hit her again at the stream, Christina thought grimly.

"Sterling's smart enough to figure out that water isn't associated with anything nice."

"But I've got to get her over water if—"

Mona's frowning eyes stopped her in mid-sentence.

Christina hung her head. "Oh, right. I'm not supposed to rush."

"Forget water for a while. Let's get your confidence back. Then we'll work on Sterling's confidence."

Exhaling loudly, Christina stood up. She was glad she'd confided in Mona. Still, it was hard to learn there was no quick and easy solution. If she couldn't get Sterling over water, she might not be able to compete in . . .

Oh, stop it! Christina scolded herself. Riding shouldn't always be about competing. She sounded like her parents. After all, raising and training horses to *win* was what their lives were all about.

After saying good-bye to Mona, she left the office and went down the aisle to Sterling's stall. The barn was quiet except for the occasional snort or rustle. Christina wondered where everyone had gone. Home, probably. Not that she blamed Melanie for heading back to Whitebrook without her. She hadn't been very nice.

When she led Sterling out of the barn, Dylan and Dakota were waiting outside. Dakota was still tacked up. Dylan had taken off his helmet. His short brown hair was damp.

Surprised, Christina didn't know what to say. Was Dylan waiting for her?

"Mind if I ride part of the way to Whitebrook with you?" Dylan asked. "Dakota needs to cool down, and it's such a nice night, and—" His voice trailed off and he ran his fingers through his hair.

"Sure!" Christina said quickly. "It's getting kind of dark. Sterling will love the company."

"Good." Dylan seemed relieved. They both mounted, then without a word headed up the hill, Dakota leading. Christina's heart began to thump. She kept telling herself that they were just two friends riding together. But if that were true, why was she so nervous?

When they reached the top of the hill, Dylan waited for Sterling to catch up so that they could ride side by side across the pasture. "What did you think of the lesson?" he asked.

"The lesson was fine, but I stunk," Christina said in a tight voice.

"Well, you like jumping better."

"True. But Mona and I talked, and I understand better why dressage is so important." She sighed. "I'm just not sure it will ever be my strong event."

"I could help you."

"You could?" Christina halted Sterling at the edge of the woods. "I mean, you would?"

"Sure. If it's okay with Mona, I could meet you here tomorrow morning."

"Wow, that'd be great," Christina exclaimed, then she caught herself. She didn't want to sound too excited. "I mean, thanks, I need all the help I can get."

Dylan gave her a big smile. "How about nine-thirty. Mona teaches a lesson at eight-thirty, so she should be finished. It won't be too hot then, or is that too early?"

"No, that's fine." Christina beamed back.

"Good. Well, I better get going. My dad's picking me up pretty soon."

"Yeah. I better hurry, too, or it's going to get dark," Christina said. Neither of them moved.

They both started laughing. Impatient to get home, Sterling began to paw and Dakota bobbed his head.

"Well, bye." Christina reluctantly steered Sterling down the path into the woods.

"Yeah, bye," Dylan said. Twisting in the saddle, Christina looked behind her. Dylan and Dakota still stood at the top of the hill.

She waved, then, her heart bursting, she squeezed Sterling into a trot and they flew the rest of the way home.

8

"DYLAN'S GOING TO HELP YOU WITH DRESSAGE?" MELANIE exclaimed. She was sitting in the grass in front of the mare and foal barn. "That is so-o-o-o cool."

"Especially since *he* asked *me*," Christina pointed out. "He even rode me partway home." She was sloshing water over Sterling's back, trying to wash off the sweat and saddle marks. It was dark, but the big lights on the outside of all the barns cast a bright glow over the stable yard.

Melanie gave Christina a devilish look. "I was wondering what took you so long to get home."

Grinning, Christina used the sweat scraper to whisk off the excess water. "Some of the time I was talking to Mona," she explained, dropping the scraper in the bucket. Then taking the towel off her shoulder, she rubbed Sterling all over.

Melanie leaned back on her elbows. "Hmm, I wonder what I could get Kevin to help me with."

"How about your catching?" Christina teased.

"Naw. I already know how to catch." Plucking a stalk of grass, Melanie stuck it in her mouth. "So what did you and Mona talk about?"

"Dressage and not rushing Sterling. The same old stuff."

"Did you tell her about Sterling's problem with water?"

"Yeah. She said to forget about it for a while and concentrate on getting my confidence back."

Melanie stared at Christina, the grass wiggling in her mouth. "Gee, I didn't know you'd lost your confidence. In fact, after you won at Foxwood you acted like you were the only one who knew what to do around horses."

She sounded so hurt that Christina quit rubbing Sterling and looked at her. "I didn't mean to."

"Is that an apology?"

"Maybe." Picking up the wet sponge off the ground, Christina threw it at Melanie. It splatted her in the chest.

"Hey!" Melanie grabbed the sponge, but by the time she threw it Christina and Sterling were jogging around the barn. Trib was already turned out in one of the small pastures. When he saw Sterling, he nickered and cantered over to the fence.

"Here's your buddy." Christina opened the gate

and led Sterling into the pasture. Unhooking the halter, she slid it off. Sterling trotted into the middle of the pasture, Trib right behind her. Bending her legs awkwardly, the mare lay down in a dusty spot. Then she rolled from side to side, kicking her hooves wildly in the air.

Christina shut the gate, then leaned on it for a minute and watched the horses. The moon was rising behind the woods, crickets chirped in the grass, and a soft breeze blew down the hill.

For the first time since Sterling refused to go in the stream, Christina felt happy. Talking to Mona had helped. Now she realized what she had to do—tackle dressage with as much zeal and determination as she tackled jumping. With lots of hard work, Sterling should be ready for the competition at Mona's.

Christina smiled to herself. And of course with Dylan helping, it wouldn't be all hard work. It was bound to be fun, too.

It was only eight-thirty when Christina got to the mare and foal barn the next morning, but Melanie was already working with Terry.

"Come watch what she can do," Melanie called as Christina passed by the weanling's stall.

"Just for a minute. I need to get over to Mona's." Setting down her grooming box, Christina looked into the stall. Because Terry was shedding out her baby hair in clumps, she looked spotted, but the new coat growing in was a glossy reddish brown. Melanie had a lead line snapped to the foal's halter. Bending at the waist, she ran her hand down Terry's front leg and said, "Foot." Immediately, Terry picked up her leg.

"Isn't that great?" Melanie said as she scraped at the small hoof with a pick. "She does that for all four feet."

"Yeah, great," Christina said absently.

Setting down the hoof, Melanie straightened. She was grinning from ear to ear. "I know. Nothing can compare to your big date with Dylan."

Christina flushed. "It's not a big date."

"Whatever. Kevin and I have a date, too."

"You do?"

"Yeah. We're going to get Terry and Rascal used to the trailer. You should bring Missy."

"And spoil your romantic moment?" she teased. "No way. I'll try Missy in the trailer later." She waved good-bye, and picking up her grooming box, headed down the aisle, stopping outside Missy's stall.

The foal raised her head, a stalk of hay sticking from her mouth. "Hey, girl," Christina said. "I'll work with you this afternoon. How's that sound?"

Missy took a step forward, her eyes big with curiosity. But when Christina reached over the door to pat her, the foal's ears went back, and she jerked out of reach.

Christina sighed. "Fine. Be that way." Turning, she went on to Sterling's stall. The last thing she felt like messing with was an ornery foal.

Fortunately, Sterling greeted her with a whiffle of pleasure. "Must be this carrot I have in my pocket," Christina said, pulling it out.

Sterling crunched happily as Christina brushed her. Humming a popular tune, she picked out her hooves and combed her tail. Christina had washed and blow-dried her own hair that morning, then Melanie had fixed it in a French braid. Not that it mattered how nice it looked. Since Mona was adamant about helmets, Dylan would never see it.

Christina led Sterling from the stall the same time Melanie came out of Terry's stall. "There's another baseball game this Saturday," Melanie said. "I think we should go."

"Me too!" Christina said enthusiastically.

Melanie looked surprised. "You do? I figured you'd say you had to work Sterling all weekend or something."

"Naw. In fact, maybe we can ask some kids to come over afterward. Have a party." The idea suddenly hit Christina and she liked it. Not only would she get to see Dylan, but it would give her a chance to spend some time with Katie, too.

"A party?" Melanie sounded totally shocked.

"Yeah. What's wrong with that?"

"Nothing. I just thought you and your friends

97

never did anything wild. Compared to what I'm used to, the summer's been kind of dullsville. Or should I say horseville? That's all anybody thinks about around here."

"You're right. And that's going to change. Tonight let's ask my mom and dad. We can invite the kids who ride at Mona's plus some of the baseball players."

"Cool." Melanie grinned. "Do you think your parents will go for it?"

"Sure. If they don't, we'll tell them how lonely you are since you left New York and how miserable you are without your father."

"I am?" Melanie frowned as if puzzled. "Oh, right, I *am*," she repeated knowingly. For a second, her mouth and shoulders drooped with sadness, then she grinned. "I can't wait to tell Kevin," she added, and clucking to Terry, she led her from the stall and down the aisle.

Christina followed with Sterling. When they got outside, Melanie hurried across the stable yard. Kevin was outside the training barn, holding Rascal. He had perched a racing saddle on the big foal's back just to see what Rascal would do.

Christina was about to mount when Sterling let out a huge whinny. Anna Simms was riding First Term from the training track. When the big colt saw Sterling, he raised his head high and bellowed a throaty reply.

"Romance must be in the air." Christina giggled. She was feeling excited and silly herself. In twenty minutes she would see Dylan again.

As she rode through the woods to Mona's, she thought about the party. Mentally, she figured out the guest list and food. But what would they do for fun? The last big party she'd had was a long-ago birthday when she was five or six. Then they'd played pin the tail on the pony and duck duck goose.

She could always ask kids to bring tapes and CDs. All her friends loved music, though a lot of the guys hated to dance. Maybe Melanie would have some more suggestions.

When they came out of the woods, Sterling broke into a jog. Christina let the mare trot across the pasture. Sterling's stride felt long and loose, and Christina hoped she'd be relaxed in the ring.

At the top of the hill, Christina sat deep and settled Sterling into a walk. Below, she could see Mona finishing up an early morning lesson with several small kids on fat ponies. The kids were trying to line their ponies up in the middle of the ring while the ponies were trying their hardest to duck out the gate. It looked like a game of tug-of-war—and the ponies were winning.

By the time Christina reached the barn, kids and ponies were spilling from the ring. Mona waved to Christina, excusing herself from several eager parents questioning her about their children's riding.

"Good morning. I'm glad to hear Dylan's going to help you," she said. "He has a good sense of what dressage is all about." Reaching behind her, she pulled some folded papers from her back pocket. "I forgot to give these to you and Melanie after the lesson yesterday."

She handed them up to Christina. "Frieda Bruder, the judge for the schooling show, is offering an eventing clinic in a couple of weeks. You take your own horse. I'm suggesting that all my students attend."

Christina unfolded the papers. "Camp Saddlebrook" was written on the front of the printed brochure.

"A riding camp?" Christina cried.

Mona smiled. "It's a little more work than your average camp. The clinic is for a variety of levels, so Melanie can go, too."

"I'll ask my mom," Christina said.

"I already mentioned it to her. She wasn't too keen on the idea of you being away for three weeks."

"Three weeks!" Christina's interest picked up. Three whole weeks of nothing but riding? It sounded great.

"Mona, may I speak to you a minute about Laralee's posting?" A worried-looking mother bustled up.

"Sure. See you later, Chris," Mona said, going off with the mother.

Refolding the brochure, Christina stuck it in her back pocket. She'd definitely ask her mom if she and Melanie could go, especially since everyone else from Mona's class was going.

I wonder if Dylan will go, she thought.

Sterling switched her tail impatiently. "Sorry, girl," Christina said. She turned the mare toward the barn. As they rode closer, Christina heard voices from inside. Then Dylan came through the doorway with Cassidy Smith and Foster, Mona's horse.

"Oh, good, you're here," Dylan said when he saw Christina. "Cassidy's going to work with us, too."

Christina's mouth fell open. "She is? I—I mean, great!" she managed to stammer. But when Dylan and Cassidy walked off together talking, Christina wanted to kick herself. How could she have been so stupid? Obviously, Dylan hadn't offered to help her because he wanted to spend time with her alone. He was just being a good friend.

Turning Sterling, Christina followed them into the ring. Dylan was giving Cassidy a leg up, his fingers linked together under her knee.

Christina gritted her teeth. *You're here for a lesson, not romance*, she reminded herself. Taking a deep breath, she rode over to join them, determined not to let her disappointment show.

"This should be fun," Cassidy said as she adjusted her stirrup. "I just wish my horses would hurry up and get here." She eyed Sterling wistfully. "Sterling looks as gorgeous as ever."

"Did you get the brochure on the eventing clinic?" Dylan asked Christina.

She nodded. "Looks like fun. I just have to convince my parents to let me go."

"I went last summer," Dylan said. "It was great. Tell your parents we're all going. Katie already signed up."

Without telling me about it? Christina felt hurt. Not that she'd seen that much of Katie lately. Between Melanie living at Whitebrook and all the time she'd been spending with Sterling, she'd neglected her best friend.

That's going to change, Christina told herself. She was going to be a better friend, starting with the party Saturday night. "Hey, how'd you guys like to get together for a party after the baseball game Saturday?" she asked.

"A party?" Cassidy's eyes lit up. "Cool."

"I'll have to take a shower first. Otherwise, I'll clear the place," Dylan said, laughing.

"No problem. We'll get together about eight."

"Who's coming? What're we going to do?" Cassidy asked.

"Oh, lots of kids," Christina said. "There will be plenty of food, and Melanie's planning some hot games like the kids play in New York."

"Sounds like summer is looking up," Dylan said. "Now let's get to work."

Fifteen minutes later, the horses had warmed up, and Dylan had them trotting small circles.

"Good, Cassidy. Foster's trot is fluid and rhythmic," Dylan called, sounding just like Mona.

What about Sterling's trot? Christina fumed silently. Of course, she knew the answer. Sterling was definitely *not* fluid or rhythmic. For the past twenty minutes, she'd trotted around the ring as if boards were nailed to her legs and neck.

"Christina, your elbows are rigid. You need to develop a following hand."

Christina rolled her eyes. She was trying, but Sterling wasn't cooperating. And the fact that Cassidy and Foster were doing great didn't help any.

Foster's an experienced event horse, Christina reminded herself. She remembered how it had felt when *she'd* ridden Foster. When Christina asked for a collected trot, Foster immediately shortened his stride, rounded his neck, and elevated his legs.

But lately when she asked Sterling to collect, the mare protested by tensing every muscle, grinding her teeth, and rooting her head. In response, Christina stiffened her own body, so they ended up fighting each other.

"Let's try a canter," Dylan suggested. "Cassidy, you go first."

Without hesitation, Foster picked up a soft, balanced canter. As Christina watched them go past, she had to admit they looked great together. So great that if Cassidy rode Foster at Saturday's dressage competition, she'd probably win.

"Okay, Chris."

Christina gave Sterling the signal to canter. The mare leaped forward as if startled. Her stride was so awkward and rough, Christina lost her balance and fell onto the mare's neck. As if it were the cue to race, Sterling flattened her ears, stretched out her neck, and really began to run.

"Whoa," Christina gasped. But Sterling was galloping wildly toward Foster.

Oh no! She thinks this is a race!

"Turn her in a small circle!" Dylan hollered.

Propping her left hand against Sterling's neck, Christina sat back and began to haul on the right rein. Sterling flew past Foster, then abruptly swerved into the center of the ring, charging straight for Dylan!

9

"LOOK OUT!" CHRISTINA HEARD CASSIDY SCREAM.

With a yelp, Dylan dove out of the way. Christina yanked hard, forcing Sterling into a tighter circle. Slowly, the mare shortened her stride, then broke into a trot.

As Christina caught her breath, she looked over to see if Dylan was okay. He was picking himself up out of the dirt.

"Are you hurt?" Cassidy trotted Foster over to him. Bending, Dylan swiped at the dirt and sand covering his jeans. "I'm fine."

"Whoa." Sitting deep, Christina pulled on the reins, forcing Sterling to halt. Then she made her back up three steps and stand. The mare was blowing loudly, her nostrils flaring with each puff.

"I'm so sorry, Dylan!" Christina exclaimed.

"Sterling must have thought she was racing in the Kentucky Derby."

"And she would have won, too," Dylan said, frowning.

Christina gulped. He was really mad. Not that she blamed him. She'd almost run him over with an out-of-control horse. Then his mouth slowly turned up in a grin. "Lighten up, Chris. Actually, it was pretty funny."

"Oh, right." Christina forced a smile. She didn't think it was funny at all. She'd been looking forward to working with Dylan. But from the time she'd arrived at Mona's, nothing had gone right. She had to face it—the lesson had been a total failure.

Just then, a van rumbled up the drive. Frightened by the loud motor, Sterling spun to face it.

"My horses are here!" Cassidy whooped. Turning Foster, she trotted from the ring.

"You want to try cantering again?" Dylan asked Christina, but his attention was on the van.

"No. I'm going to trot her quietly until she's settled down."

"Good idea. Then how about a lesson tomorrow?" he asked, glancing her way briefly before looking back at the van. Christina could hear the hesitation in his voice. Not that she blamed him. Cassidy had told them so much about her horses, Christina was dying to see them, too.

"Maybe another day," Christina said, but Dylan was already walking toward the barn.

The van halted in front of the double doors. Mona came out of her office and took Foster from Cassidy. She was so excited, she was hopping from foot to foot.

Christina steered Sterling closer. The driver jumped from the cab. Cassidy obviously knew the man, since she started chattering excitedly to him while they lowered the heavy ramp on the side of the van.

"They traveled well, Ms. Smith," the man was saying. "But they'll be ready for a roll and some turnout time."

"Oh, I can't wait to see them again. It seems like forever."

The man handed Cassidy a lead line and she followed him up the ramp. Christina could hear Cassidy cooing and talking baby talk, then the man led out one of the horses.

It was a light gray gelding. He was covered with a cooler, but Christina could tell he was bigger-boned and at least a hand taller than Sterling. Still, the two horses looked similar. No wonder Cassidy had been attracted to Sterling.

Then Cassidy led the second horse down the ramp, and Christina caught her breath. Since Mona evented, her horses were built more for athletic ability than beauty. But Cassidy's horse looked as perfect as one of the winning conformation hunters pictured in the *Chronicle of the Horse*.

At the bottom of the ramp, the horse stopped and looked around. He had an alert, regal expression, and his mahogany-colored coat gleamed in the sun.

"Wow," Christina said under her breath. Sterling fidgeted, then nickered a greeting to the two new horses. Cassidy led her horse toward an empty paddock next to the barn, the man following with the big gray. Dylan, Mona, and Foster trailed behind them.

Christina heaved a sigh. Suddenly, she didn't even feel like trotting Sterling. Maybe she had better just head home.

She left the ring, and as she rode from the farm she decided that from now on she'd work Sterling alone. The mare acted too crazy when she was in the ring with other horses. A week working in a field with no one else around might help solve their dressage problems.

And Christina needed to solve their problems. Mona had said that she needed to get her confidence back. But it seemed as though everything she was doing was making it worse. First she'd made mistakes over water and now she was having trouble on the flat. How could she and Sterling suddenly be so terrible at this dressage stuff?

She thought back to the test they'd ridden at Foxwood. Their score hadn't been the best, but it hadn't been the worst, either. Maybe that was because she'd been so excited to ride, she'd been in a daze. Plus, since it was a novice test, the horse could move freely. Collection seemed to be what made Sterling so tense. When Christina used her seat and rein to ask the mare to flex her poll, round her back, and bring her hind legs under her, Sterling resisted.

Mona had explained why. Sterling was a racehorse used to stretching out, and pulling on the reins meant "race." Still, Christina *had* to get her lighter and more collected before they could move up to training level. She just wished she knew how.

As they rode into the woods, sweat trickled down Christina's cheek. It was after ten-thirty, the sun was high, and the air was sticky and thick. Deerflies swarmed around Christina's head and Sterling's neck. Stopping, Christina stripped a leafy branch from a tree to swoosh them away. Then she turned her thoughts to something happier. *The party.*

Her parents just had to say yes. After all, Melanie needed to meet some of the other kids. She should have asked them last night, but they'd been busy with a new client. As soon as she got home, she'd ask them. A party this weekend would help take her mind off riding.

When Christina rode down the hill toward Whitebrook, she heard thumping and clattering coming from the van parked behind the mare and foal barn. She grinned. Melanie and Kevin must be having their big date.

Head high, Sterling slowly approached the van

until a loud bang made her stop dead. Patting the mare's neck, Christina reassured her it was all right. "Don't worry. It's not ghosts."

When they'd ridden around the cab to the van's side door, Christina hollered, "Melanie! Say something so Sterling knows it's you in there and not some monster."

"It's not some monster!" Melanie hollered back. Then she stuck her head out the open door. With her striped hair sticking up, she almost looked like a ghoul.

"How are they doing?" Christina asked.

"Great. Terry went right up the ramp and backed into the stall. I gave her lots of treats, and now she thinks the van is a fun place to be."

Just then Kevin and Rascal appeared at the top of the ramp. Rascal whinnied at Sterling, his neigh shrill and babyish. His big brown eyes were wide with apprehension.

"How about Rascal?"

"Well, at first he decided there was no way he was going up that ramp." Kevin scratched under the foal's forelock. "But once Terry went up, he followed. He didn't want some female outdoing him."

Melanie rolled her eyes. "You mean, *you* didn't want some female outdoing you," she corrected.

Christina laughed.

Kevin looked sheepish. "Well, I have to admit, Melanie, you're doing a great job with your weanling."

"Thank you." Melanie grinned, pleased. Then she turned her attention back to Christina. "How'd your lesson go?"

Christina groaned. "I don't want to talk about it. Did you mention the party to Kevin?"

"She did, and I think it's a great idea," Kevin said.

"Good. Now we have to convince my parents."

Kevin's jaw dropped. "You haven't told them yet?"

"No." Christina wrinkled her nose. Kevin knew what her parents were like. They were so busy with the farm, it was hard to get them to make time for anything else.

"I'm sure they'll say it's okay, especially since Melanie and I will do everything."

Melanie snorted. "Oh, right, like I've hosted lots of parties."

"Haven't you?"

"No. I've been to a lot of neat bashes, but my dad's always too busy to have people over to our place."

"Well, at least you know what food to serve and games to play—stuff like that."

"Chips and soda? Hide-and-seek?" Melanie joked.

"Just getting together with friends will be fun," Kevin said as he led Rascal down the ramp. "Summer's half over." The weanling cautiously put one foot in front of the other until he was almost at the end. Then he gathered his hind legs under him and leaped.

111

"Easy." Kevin swung him around, then waited for Melanie to lead Terry from the van. As Christina watched, she had to admit that Melanie was doing a super job. She was patient and gentle, and Terry seemed to trust her already.

"Melanie, I want you with me when I talk to my mom," Christina said. "If you look forlorn enough, she'll have to say yes."

"Okay. I need to put Terry away first."

Kevin and Melanie headed back to the barn with their weanlings. They walked side by side, talking excitedly about the party. Following behind them, Christina felt left out.

She and Dylan were definitely not hitting it off. Even though Kevin insisted that Dylan liked her, he and Cassidy seemed awfully close. When Sterling had almost run him over, he'd been a good sport, but Christina could tell that he'd been disappointed in the lesson. Disappointed in *her*. Not that she blamed him. She was disappointed in herself, too. She used to think she was a rider who could handle just about anything.

Still, she really liked Dylan. Maybe they could have a second chance at the party.

When she reached the barn, Christina dismounted, untacked Sterling, and washed her. She was walking down the aisle, cooling Sterling off, when Melanie caught up with her.

"Ready to ask your mom?" she asked as she fell into step beside Christina.

112

"I am. Though I don't have a clue where she is."

Clapping a hand to her mouth, Melanie stifled a giggle.

Christina gave her an odd look. "What's so funny?"

"Nothing," Melanie said, then grinned mysteriously.

"What?" Christina prodded. Halting Sterling, she faced her cousin.

Melanie glanced around as if making sure nobody were listening, then whispered. "Kevin said he'd come over and get me before we start the party. You know, like it's a date."

Christina grinned. "You're kidding! Kevin?"

"Yup. Maybe Dylan will ask you."

"Not after today's lesson." Christina let out a big sigh.

"Uh-oh. That bad?"

"Worse. Sterling almost ran him over."

Melanie's eyes widened in disbelief, then she burst out laughing. "That's one way to get a guy—flatten him so he can't get away."

"Mel!" Christina fumed, then burst out laughing, too. After checking to make sure Sterling was cool, she put her in her stall. She fed Sterling a flake of hay and made sure the horse had water. Then she joined Melanie, who was waiting outside Trib's stall.

"I'm glad you let me ride him the other day," she

113

told Christina. "Pirate's great as a lead pony, but he'll never be able to do anything else. And so far, Trib and I have gotten along great."

"I agree. Hey!" Christina remembered the brochure in her pocket. She pulled it out. "Mona gave me this. It's a three-week eventing clinic where we stay at this farm."

"Only I don't know how to event."

"We're all learning. Besides, Mona says it's for different levels. We can ask Mom if you can take Trib."

Melanie's eyes brightened. "Cool." Then she giggled. "If I'm not careful, I'm going to be as horse-crazy as you."

"That's not so terrible." Linking her arm with Melanie's, Christina steered her down the aisle. "Come on. Let's find my mom."

Christina crossed her fingers, hoping that her mother would say yes. She knew that when Ashleigh was busy with training and racing, she sometimes had a one-track mind. *Kind of like me*, Christina thought.

"Let's check the stallion barn," Melanie suggested. Breaking into a jog, the two girls ran down the worn path in the grass to the smaller barn that housed Whitebrook's six stallions.

The barn was dark and cooled by ceiling fans. As they went down the aisle, Christina hunted for signs that her mother or father was around. But the barn was quiet. Breeding season was pretty much over, and the furious activity of spring had died down.

As they passed the stalls, Christina said hi to the various stallions, stopping in front of Blues King's door. It had been a while since she'd been in the barn, and she missed seeing her father's Thoroughbred stallion who'd become gentle as a kitten in his old age.

"They're not here. I'll check in the training barn," Melanie called as she went ahead. Suddenly, Christina heard a loud crash, and Melanie screamed.

"What happened?" Christina cried, but when she saw Melanie standing frozen in the middle of the aisle, a look of horror on her face, she knew the answer. "Did Terminator scare you to death?"

"I thought he was coming through the door!" Melanie gasped, her palm flattened against her heart.

Christina hurried over to her. Terminator stood behind his closed door, staring at them with a look of fierce hatred. He was a handsome gray stallion, but his disposition was so ugly that the only one who worked with him was George Ballard, the manager of the stallion barn.

Pinning his ears, the Terminator came at them again, clashing his bared teeth against the metal mesh of the door. Christina shuddered. "Come on." She tugged on Melanie's arm. "Let's get out of here before George comes in and thinks we're teasing him."

They rushed from the stallion barn and across the

stable yard to the training barn. Even though it was midmorning, the place still bustled with activity—grooms brushing horses and stablehands mucking stalls. Outside an open stall door, Christina spotted her father leaning against the door frame, looking into the stall.

"There's Dad. Maybe he knows where Mom is."

"Hey, Chris. Hey, Melanie," her father greeted them. Wrapping his arm around Christina's shoulder, he gave her a squeeze. "I haven't seen much of you today. You rushed out of the house so fast this morning."

"I went to Mona's for a lesson." Christina leaned against her dad. He smelled like sweat, horses, and fresh air. He wore a short-sleeved shirt and jeans that were already rumpled and dusty from working around the barn. Still, Christina thought he looked handsome.

Peering into the stall, Christina saw her mom stooping next to a young horse. It took her a second to realize it was First Term. A groom stood by his head, his one hand clutching a lead rope, the other holding the cheekpiece of his halter.

"What's going on?" Christina asked.

Ashleigh stood up. Her cheeks were flushed from the heat and her brow was furrowed with lines of frustration. "His leg's really hot. It might be a mild bow. I better call Dr. Lanum and have her do a sonogram."

Mike blew out his breath. "Even if it's mild, it'll set back his training for months."

"I should have known it would happen." Ashleigh shook her head as if angry at herself. "He was just too big, too young, and too full of himself. We should have waited."

When she came out of the stall, Ashleigh noticed the girls. "What are you two up to?"

"Umm." One look at her mother's face and Christina knew this wasn't a good time to ask about the party. Even though the bow probably couldn't have been helped, her mother still took each injury personally.

"We want to ask about having a party this Saturday," Melanie said before Christina could stop her. "Just about ten kids."

Immediately, Ashleigh shook her head. "Sorry. Can't do it."

"Why not?" Christina asked.

"It's just not a good time," Ashleigh answered absently. She was already dialing the veterinarian's number on her cellular phone.

Christina couldn't believe it. Her mother hadn't even thought one second about the party before she said no! She hadn't even bothered to ask why they wanted to have a party, or to find out how important it was to Christina.

"It's not a good time?" Christina repeated. "Why? Because as usual you don't have time for something *I* want to do?"

Christina saw Melanie's surprised expression. But she didn't care if she was making a scene. All week long everything had gone wrong. She couldn't take it if her parents ruined her party plans, too.

"Now, Chris—" Mike began.

"It's not fair and you know it!" Christina interrupted her father.

Before he could respond, she spun around and fled from the barn.

10

Tearing across the stable yard, Christina ran into the mare and foal barn and down the aisle. Usually she went into the attic in the house to be alone. But this time she wanted to be with Sterling.

She threw back the latch on the stall door. Surprised, Sterling raised her head and stared at Christina with her big brown eyes. A hunk of hay hung from her mouth.

"Don't mind me," Christina mumbled. Ducking under the mare's neck, she went into the farthest corner. She kicked the straw into a pile, then dropped down on it and slumped against the wall.

Angrily, she swiped the tears from her eyes. She should have known what her mother would say. But at least Ashleigh could've listened first. Maybe if she knew how important the party was, she would have changed her mind. But her mother had just said no without even thinking about what Christina wanted.

Wrapping her arms around her knees, Christina buried her face in her arms. Sterling came over, snuffling curiously, then nuzzled her hair with velvety lips.

Christina giggled. She reached up and stroked the mare's soft nose. "You understand, don't you?"

"Christina?" She heard Melanie call.

Christina stiffened. She held her breath, trying not to make a sound, hoping Melanie wouldn't find her. Sterling shuffled back over to eat the rest of her hay, hiding Christina.

Footsteps came up the aisle. Christina huddled in the corner, making herself as small as possible. She knew Melanie would be on her side, but she didn't want to talk to anybody. When the footsteps receded and Christina was sure Melanie had gone, she let out her breath. She stood up and gave Sterling a hug.

Christina's stomach growled, but there was no way she was going back to the house for lunch. Maybe she'd take Trib for a ride in the woods and go leaping down the cross-country trail. But the thought of the deerflies and heat dissuaded her.

Going over to the door, she checked the aisle to make sure Melanie had gone. Her gaze landed on the three stalls where the weanlings were kept.

That's what she needed to do to take her mind off everything—work with Missy.

After saying good-bye to Sterling, she went into the tack room for her grooming box and headed to Missy's stall. The foal was dozing in the corner. When she heard the door being opened, she raised her head, instantly alert.

"Hey, girl. It's just me," Christina said, keeping her voice calm. When she went into the stall, Christina left the door partway open just in case she had to jump out of the way of Missy's flying hooves.

Holding out her hand, Christina let the foal sniff it. Missy's ears flicked back and forth as if she weren't sure whether to be suspicious, mean, or friendly. Talking softly, Christina inched closer and closer until she was able to catch hold of the halter. Instantly, Missy threw her head up and stepped back. Christina moved with her, trying not to pull on the halter. When the weanling stopped, Christina used her free hand to stroke her neck.

"See? It's not so bad, is it?" she asked as she snapped the lead line onto the halter. Missy eyed her warily. Reaching down, Christina scooped a brush from the box. The same instant, Missy whirled, pulling the lead from Christina's grasp. Then she kicked, her back hoof hitting Christina squarely in the thigh.

With a cry of pain, Christina staggered back, slamming into the stall wall. Missy spied the open door and in one jump was through it and free.

"Whoa!" Christina hollered, but by the time she limped to the door Missy was gone.

"*Arrgh!*" She gave a cry of frustration and pain. Unzipping her jeans, she peeled them far enough down to check her leg. The skin wasn't broken, but already it was turning black and blue.

Christina hobbled down the aisle. Her face was flaming with anger and embarrassment. How could she have been so stupid! She should have known the little beast would make a break for it.

Christina knew she had to hurry and catch Missy. The foal could easily hurt herself. Besides, Christina didn't want anyone to find out what had happened.

When she got outside, the sun was so bright it made her eyes water. She looked right, then left, hoping to see Missy cropping grass quietly. But the foal was nowhere in sight.

Christina rubbed her temples. Her head ached, her thigh pounded, she was furious, and the only person she could blame was herself.

Exhaling loudly, she headed around the barn to the pastures. When she didn't see Missy, Christina's stomach knotted with worry. Where could the foal have gone?

Fortunately, Whitebrook had fences all around it so that if a horse did get lose it couldn't escape to the road. Still, a foal could find a million ways to get in trouble.

Christina limped to the stallion barn, checking behind it before going down the aisle. Terminator threw himself at the door in a mock attack, making a huge racket, but other than that the building was quiet.

When she got outside, Christina stood and scanned the area. The backyard, drive, stable area, and paddocks were empty. The knot in her stomach tightened.

"There you are!"

Christina looked over her shoulder. Melanie was jogging down the aisle, giving Terminator's stall a wide berth. "I've been looking everywhere for you."

Too miserable to respond, Christina started for the training barn.

"Are you all right?" Melanie asked as she hurried after her.

"Yes."

"Then wait up."

Sighing, Christina halted.

"You're not all right. You're limping. What happened?"

"Missy kicked me." Christina started off again. "Now she's loose and I have to find her."

"Loose!" Melanie exclaimed. "How'd she get—"

Without breaking stride, Christina glared at her. Melanie shut her mouth.

"Okay. I won't ask," she said a minute later. "Did you check everywhere?"

"I haven't checked the training barn. I was afraid I'd run into my mother."

This time Melanie didn't say anything, and Christina was grateful. When they reached the barn,

Christina hesitated before going inside. She could see the vet's truck parked at the other end. That meant her mom and dad would be inside.

Melanie touched her shoulder. "Hey. I'll go in and look."

"You will?"

"Sure. I've had to ask friends to cover for me lots of times. You check around back."

"Thanks," Christina said as Melanie went in. She hobbled around the corner, hoping to see Missy's ornery little face peering at her from around a fence post or tree. But there was no sign of the foal.

Stopping at the other end by the vet's truck, Christina rested her throbbing leg. If she ever caught the little beast, she'd . . .

Melanie came out, shaking her head. "She's not there."

"Where could she be?" Christina felt her throat thicken. She swallowed hard, not wanting to cry. She'd really blown it today. How was she going to explain a lost foal on top of everything else?

"She's got to be somewhere," Melanie said, patting Christina awkwardly on the back. "I know—let's think like a foal."

Christina made a scoffing noise. "That's dumb."

"You have any other ideas?" Melanie retorted.

Christina shook her head. "No. And I'm sorry I snapped at you. I'm just mad at myself. Actually, your idea's a good one."

"Apology accepted." Melanie tapped her chin as if thinking hard. "Now if I were a foal, where would I go?" Suddenly, her eyes popped wide. "I know!" Grabbing Christina's hand, Melanie dragged her around the vet's truck toward the mare and foal barn.

"But I checked there already," Christina protested.

Melanie didn't slow down. She pulled Christina into the barn, stopping in front of a dark stall. "I bet you didn't check here!"

The door was half open. Christina peered inside. Missy was standing against the far side wall, the lead line still dangling from her halter.

"How'd you know she'd be in there?" Christina asked in amazement, but then a horse's head appeared behind the bars in the top half of the partition between the stalls. Raising her own head, Missy gave a throaty whinny and the horse next door immediately answered.

Christina inhaled sharply. "That's Miss America, her mother!"

"Right. I knew there was an empty stall next to her. I thought maybe Missy might have gone looking for her."

Missy was pressed against the wall, trying to get as close to her mother as she could. "Oh, look at her." Christina's heart melted, and her anger disappeared. "I thought she was a little witch. But all this time, she's been pining away for her mother. Ian always said some foals take separation a lot harder than others."

"Obviously, Missy was one of them," Melanie agreed.

Entering slowly, Christina approached the foal. This time, she stood quietly. Christina caught the dangling lead line, then scratched Missy's fuzzy mane. The foal wiggled her lips with delight.

For a second, Christina just stood there, wondering what to do. Missy had to be weaned from her mother. She had to get used to human contact, too. But maybe there was another way Christina could do it that wouldn't be quite so rough on the foal.

"You know, I think Terry missed her mother, too," Melanie said. "But I spent so much time with her, maybe she didn't get so lonely."

And I didn't spend enough time with Missy, Christina thought. But that was going to change.

"I wish I had done that." Unsnapping the lead line, Christina let the foal loose. "I'm going to leave her in here. I'll switch her bucket and feed tub. Maybe after a few days of working with her here, she'll be quiet enough to move back with the others."

Melanie furrowed her brow. "Don't you think you better check with your mom before you do something like that?"

"I will." Christina took a deep breath. "And I'll tell her my reasons, too." *And hopefully she'll understand and respect them.*

Melanie nodded. Christina changed tubs and buckets. When the stall was ready, they watched Missy for a few more minutes. She was like a different foal. Even though she couldn't see her mother, she could smell her, and she'd settled down and was contentedly munching hay.

Christina let out a sigh, suddenly realizing how worn out she was. She was hot, sticky, tired, and her leg hurt. "I think I've had enough horse stuff for today," she told Melanie. "I'm going in for lunch and a shower."

"Sounds good. What do you want to do then?"

"Do you have some of those cool posters your dad sent you?"

Melanie nodded.

"Good. Let's work on redecorating my room."

Not bad, Christina thought as she looked around her room. It was almost dinnertime. She and Melanie had spent several hours fooling around with different ideas. Christina had taken down the rest of the fluffy curtains, leaving the white shades. They'd rearranged the furniture. They'd chosen three posters with brightly colored backgrounds and tacked them on the wall. Then they'd stripped the flowered spread and dust ruffle off the bed.

Christina liked the posters and the way they'd moved the furniture. But the bed looked bare. It needed something.

Going into the hall, Christina went down to the bathroom. Melanie was taking a bubble bath. She had a boom box blaring and was singing at the top of her lungs.

"Mel!" Christina knocked on the door. When the singing grew louder, she pounded harder. "Melanie! Can you hear me?"

"You know that I looooove youuuuuu!"

"I guess not," Christina muttered. She was hoping Melanie might have an idea about the bed. She wanted the room to look nice before her mother saw it.

Christina had no idea what her mother would say. All week, Ashleigh had been so busy at the barn she hadn't even noticed that Christina had taken down one set of curtains. But now the room looked so different she had to notice, and when she did, Christina wanted it to look just right.

The attic! Christina often hung out in the attic when she was feeling blue. It was full of boxes and chests, and there was an old quilt that covered Christina's favorite chair. The quilt was too musty and worn for her bedroom, but Christina bet there was something else she could use.

She hurried up the steps, closing the attic door behind her. The tiny room was stifling, and sweat popped out on her brow. She hurried to the chest. When she opened it, she smelled the pungent odor of cedar. Several winter coats lay folded on top. Rooting around underneath them, Christina found what looked like another quilt. She pulled it out.

It was beautiful—interconnecting rings of gingham patches sewn together with tiny stitches. There were a few frays and rips, but Christina still loved it. She wondered why it was kept in the chest, then decided she didn't care. It belonged on her bed.

Closing up the chest, she took the quilt downstairs. It needed a good airing out, but she wanted to see how it looked first. She smoothed it over her mattress, then stepped back. The rings of colors against the white background looked perfect in her room.

"Where did you get that?"

Christina turned. Ashleigh stood in the doorway, staring at the quilt. Her face and clothes were streaked with sweat and dirt.

"The attic."

For a minute, Ashleigh didn't say anything. She walked slowly into the room, and reaching down, ran her palm along the quilt. "It was my grandmother's. I'd forgotten about it." Straightening, she studied the rest of the room.

Christina's palms started to sweat. What would her mother say about the new look? *Why should I care so much?* she wondered.

Christina recalled how angry she was when her mother vetoed the party and how anxious she was when Missy got loose. Suddenly she felt tired—tired of worrying about what her parents thought. "I decided my room needed redoing," Christina declared. "I found the quilt in the cedar chest. I think it looks great on my bed."

Ashleigh glanced at Christina and gave her a small smile. "It looks nice. Your whole room looks nice," she added. "Look, Christina, about the party . . ."

Christina wasn't sure she wanted to hear any more about the party. Picking up the curtains, she began folding them.

"I didn't mean to sound so negative," Ashleigh explained. "You caught me at a bad time. First Term's leg is pretty messed up."

"I understand," Christina mumbled, though she didn't. What did a racehorse's problems have to do with her own?

"The only reason you can't have a party this Saturday is because your dad and I are already attending the Racing Association Dinner. But how about next Saturday after the show at Mona's? You and your friends can celebrate how well you did."

"No, that's a terrible idea." Christina shook her head fiercely. Didn't her mother get it? Mona's show would be a disaster. The only thing she and Sterling would have to celebrate was coming in dead last.

Suddenly, all the problems of the past week came crashing in on Christina. Her eyes welled with tears.

Ashleigh gasped. "What's wrong?"

Hurrying over, she slipped her arm around her

daughter's shoulders. Tears rolled down Christina's cheeks and her body began to shake. Turning, she buried her face against her mother's chest.

"Oh, Mom," she choked out. "You have no idea. I've messed everything up—Dylan, Sterling, Missy—and it's all my fault!"

11

"EVERYTHING?" ASHLEIGH REPEATED.

Christina nodded, her chin scraping against the buttons of her mother's shirt. Ashleigh led her to the bed. Side by side, the two of them sat on the quilt.

"Why didn't you tell me before?" Ashleigh asked, handing her a tissue.

Christina blew her nose, honking loudly. "I wanted to figure out what to do myself. And you were always so . . . so . . . ," her voice faded.

"Busy," Ashleigh finished. "I'm sorry." Her own eyes filled with tears.

Reaching over to the bedside table, Christina pulled a tissue from the box and handed it to her mother. "Here."

Ashleigh dabbed her eyes. "Thanks. Now tell me everything."

Christina took a shaky breath, then began. She told her mother about Sterling, her problems with dressage and water, the horrible lesson with Dylan, and losing Missy.

"It seems like I've done everything wrong," Christina said. "Like with Missy. I thought she was mean and ornery, but she just missed her mother."

Ashleigh smiled gently. "Sounds like someone else I know."

"Who?" Christina frowned, puzzled. Then she realized Ashleigh was talking about herself. "No, it's not the same," Christina said quickly.

"Isn't it? You're growing up, you want to be independent, and yet you still need your mom—at least a *little* bit," she added, giving Christina a hug. "And your mom hasn't really been around much these past few weeks. Don't you think that's been part of your problem?"

Christina thought about it. She *had* missed having her mom's attention lately. It had made her feel as if she had to solve all her problems without any help at all. Slowly, she nodded. "Maybe you're right." She grinned up at Ashleigh, feeling a little better. "At least about *that*. But what about everything else?"

"It sounds like you figured out what to do with Missy. Leaving her next to her mother until she gets used to you is a good idea."

"I guess." Christina sat up a little straighter.

"As for the other problems . . ." Ashleigh shook

her head. "I wish I had all the answers, but I don't. All I know is that everything important takes time—and that goes for relationships with boys as well as horses. When you first bought Sterling, you had big dreams of eventing. Only you forgot that horses have minds and feelings, too. Sterling wasn't ready to handle your big dreams."

"But I still kept pushing her," Christina admitted sadly.

"Now you have to rethink the situation, just like I had to do with First Term. I've decided to take him totally out of training until next spring."

"Wow. That must have been a hard decision."

"It was, considering he could have raced this fall. But if I push him, he could also break down and be ruined for the rest of his life."

"So what does that have to do with my problem with Sterling?"

"If your dream is eventing at training level *right now*, then maybe you need to get an older well-trained horse who's ready to compete."

"You mean sell Sterling!" Christina's eyes widened.

"I didn't say that. But if she's not the right horse, then you have to decide what to do. You might want to sell her, or you might want to lease a seasoned horse until Sterling's ready."

"Oh." Christina chewed her lip. She understood what her mother was saying. Still, just as after her talk with Mona, she wished there was a quick, easy solution.

"Hey." Tipping up her chin, Ashleigh looked her in the eyes. "One thing you have to remember, Chris, is that making tough decisions isn't easy. Sometimes it takes a lot of courage."

Christina nodded sadly.

"Now," Ashleigh continued. "About Mona's show and having a party afterward—just remember that it shouldn't matter if you win or lose. What matters is how hard you try, right?"

Christina nodded again, though it was easier to say than do. She'd have a tough time getting in the party mood after spending the day making a fool out of herself in front of a judge, her instructor, and all her friends.

Still, now she knew that the show and the party would be the easy part. Her mother was right. She had to think hard about her horse and her dreams, and if Sterling wasn't the right horse she'd have to have the courage to decide what to do.

"Go, Kevin!" Melanie, Christina, and Beth McLean whooped as Kevin raced from first to third. The first baseman threw the ball. Kevin barreled toward second, sliding in a swirl of dust just as the second baseman caught the ball and tagged him.

"Out!" the field umpire hollered.

Groaning loudly, Beth and Christina dropped back onto the bleachers. Saturday's game was not going well. Melanie pumped her fist in the air. "He was safe!"

Grabbing onto the hem of her cousin's T-shirt, Christina dragged her down onto the seat. "Do you want to get us thrown out?"

"No, but he was safe!" Melanie exclaimed.

"Dylan's up," Beth said, her voice tense. It was the last inning, and the Blue Jays were down by one run. They had one man on third and two outs.

"Hit a homer, Dylan. All we need is one run to tie!" Melanie called.

Christina crossed her fingers. "Come on, Dylan," she whispered.

Dylan got ready to bat, an intense look on his face. Christina held her breath as the Jets' pitcher threw the ball over home plate.

"Strike one!"

Melanie popped off the bleachers. "Strike? What're you talking—"

Beth and Christina jerked her back down.

"If you say one more word, I'm going to shove my sandal in your mouth," Christina warned.

Melanie's eyes widened. "You wouldn't."

"Strike two!"

Christina clutched the edge of the bleachers. If Dylan struck out now, they'd lose!

As the pitcher wound up, her fingers gripped the

seat even tighter. He threw the ball. In slow motion, it flew toward Dylan. He swung, the bat slicing through the air, missing the ball. It smacked into the catcher's mitt.

"Strike three!"

The home team fans groaned. The Jets' fans went wild.

Dylan dropped his chin to his chest. Shoulders slumped, he slunk back to the dugout.

"Well, that stunk," Melanie muttered.

Christina felt like a deflated balloon. She could not imagine how horrible Dylan must be feeling.

Ever since the lesson, she'd avoided him. Melanie and Kevin had practically forced her to come to the game. She was glad she had. He might need a friend.

"I'm going to find Kevin." Jumping off the bleachers, Melanie disappeared in the departing crowd.

"I'll wait for you guys by the car," Beth said. She'd given them a ride from Whitebrook.

"Okay." Christina sat down, wondering what to say to Dylan. "Sorry about the strikeout"? "Gee, at least you tried"?

They both sounded so dumb.

Standing up, she tried to spot Dylan over the sea of heads. The coach had finished talking to the team, but Dylan was still seated in the dugout, stuffing his bat and glove in his bag.

Then he stood up and slung his bag over his shoulder. "Nice strikeout," someone teased.

Realizing it was now or never, Christina jumped off the bleachers. "Hey, Dylan," she called as she approached the dugout.

He glanced over his shoulder. "Hey."

"Are you okay?"

"Sure." He shrugged. "It's not the first time I've struck out."

"Right." Christina smiled hesitantly. "I just thought—"

"That I'd feel like dirt?" he guessed.

"Sort of."

"Well, I feel worse than dirt. I feel like horse manure."

Christina bit back a laugh. "That's pretty awful. And I should know. Can I buy you a soda?" She fished in the pocket of her shorts.

"Sure. Why not." Slinging the bag off his shoulder, he dropped it on the picnic table. Christina went over to the concession stand, paid for two sodas, and brought them over. Without opening the can, Dylan held it against his forehead. "Ahh. That feels good. I'm about a hundred degrees."

"I guess it's just as well I didn't have the party tonight," Christina said.

"Why not?"

"You and Kevin wouldn't feel much like celebrating."

"Because we lost?"

"Right."

"Hey, it's just a game."

Christina frowned. "You're not down?"

"For a minute or two. I mean, no one wants to make the last out, but somebody has to. It might as well be me."

"Wow. I wish I could be like that. I get so down on myself."

"I noticed." He popped the top on the can and took a sip.

"I mean, I didn't want to have the party next Saturday after the dressage show because I knew Sterling and I probably wouldn't do so hot."

"If you don't do well, that's when you *really* need to get together with friends."

Christina smiled. "You're right."

Circle left. Sitting trot to K. *Canter at* K. Christina recited to herself as she put Sterling through a practice novice test. She was on top of the hill in one of the pastures. Black letters painted on cardboard were tacked on fence posts, trees, and stakes. The area wasn't perfectly flat and the letters weren't posted in the exact spots as they would be in a real dressage arena, but Christina didn't care.

Since her lesson with Dylan several days ago, she'd worked Sterling alone—on the trail, in the pastures, and now in her makeshift arena. The solitary rides had helped them both. Sterling was more relaxed and responsive, until Christina asked for something the mare didn't want to do—like a slow canter or a collected trot. Then the old resistance came back.

Sterling would stiffen her neck and hollow her back. Her gaits would become so choppy that Christina bounced awkwardly, only making things worse.

This morning wasn't any better. At the free walk from *K* to *M*, Sterling hung her head so low that Christina almost quit. But she persisted, gathering the reins and finishing with a trot down the center line. Halting, she saluted a pretend judge.

Then she collapsed in the saddle. Tomorrow was Saturday, the day of the dressage competition at Mona's. They were going to stink.

"Well, that was torture," she muttered to Sterling. The mare snorted dust and dirt from her nostrils, looking nearly as dejected as Christina felt. Letting the reins hang slack, Christina turned Sterling into the woods for a cool-down walk.

They ambled down the path, Sterling cocking her ears at the rippling shadows made by the sun through the canopy of trees. Christina tried to enjoy the pretty morning, but a nagging question kept buzzing through her head: What was she going to do about Sterling?

She'd taken care of her other problems. The party was set for tomorrow evening after the show. She and Melanie had planned hamburgers and hot dogs on the grill. This afternoon, Melanie was baking a cake, and Christina was making potato and fruit salads. And for fun, they'd told everybody to wear bathing suits and shorts. Kevin had borrowed squirt guns and Super Soakers from his friends. Tomorrow afternoon, they were filling up balloons, buckets, and an old wading pool with water.

And Missy was doing much better. Christina had worked with her several times a day all weekend and this week. Stroking her back legs with the whip had gotten her used to being touched, and now Christina could rub her all over with her hands.

Yesterday, she'd moved Missy back to her old stall. The weanling had nickered sadly for her mother, but as soon as Christina started grooming her, she'd settled down. Still, they had a long way to go. Christina hadn't tried to load her or pick up her feet, but at least they were making progress.

And as for Dylan . . . Christina smiled happily. She hadn't seen him since the baseball game, but he'd called a couple of times just to talk.

So the only problem left was Sterling.

Christina knew Sterling had the athletic potential to event. But did she have the heart and spirit? What if her resisting got worse? Then Christina would always have trouble getting Sterling to do anything

142

she didn't like. Successful event horses had to be bold and confident, yet trusting. Otherwise, their riders would never get them around the long, tough cross-country courses.

Reaching down, Christina stroked the mare's neck. Her coat was smooth and silky, and the dapples shone in the sparkling light. When Christina first set eyes on Sterling, she'd fallen in love with her. But was that enough? What about her own dreams of eventing?

Looking up, Christina suddenly realized they'd gone deep into the woods. Up ahead the path split. If they went right, it would take them to Mona's. If they went left, it would lead to the stream.

Sterling went left.

Christina's fingers tightened on the reins. It was almost as if Sterling knew about Christina's dilemma.

No, that's crazy. Still, Christina decided to let her go down to the water. It had been almost two weeks since she'd tried to ride Sterling over the stream. It was time she tried again.

"Please go in, Sterling," Christina whispered. All she needed was a little sign that the mare trusted her enough to try.

Heart thumping, Christina stopped about three feet from the rushing water. "There it is," she said, nodding her chin toward the stream. "The horrible place where sharks, stingrays, and trolls live. Maybe even the Loch Ness monster."

Stretching out her neck, Sterling blew loudly as if she believed every word. Christina squeezed her calves against the mare's sides, urging her forward. Sterling took one baby step, then another.

Christina tensed excitedly. *She was going to do it!*

Then Sterling stopped dead.

"Just one more step," Christina pleaded. But Sterling switched her tail, rolled her eyes, and flattened her ears.

Christina let out a shaky breath. She knew that stubborn look. Sterling wasn't going to budge.

"Oh, Sterling." A rush of disappointment and sadness overwhelmed Christina. Leaning over the pommel, she threw her arms around the mare's neck and sobbed into the soft mane until she couldn't cry anymore.

When her sobs subsided, Christina realized that she had made her decision.

"Sterling, you're as stubborn and pigheaded as an old mule," she snuffled. "But I love you, anyway. Even if you never go in the water or jump another liverpool, you're the only horse I want."

Sitting up, she wiped her nose on her sleeve. "I'll just have to figure out a new dream."

There. She'd made her decision. Christina hiccuped, then smiled. She couldn't believe how much better she felt. It was as if a huge weight had lifted off her heart.

Reaching down, she rubbed Sterling's withers.

"Maybe we could try barrel racing or calf roping," she suggested, half joking. "What do you think of that?"

With a shake of her mane, Sterling stepped forward. Her front hoof landed in the stream. She snorted suspiciously.

Then, to Christina's astonishment, she lowered her head, touched the water with velvety lips, and began to drink.

12

"YOU LOOK GREAT, MELANIE," CHRISTINA SAID. HER COUSIN was wearing the black hunt coat, white riding breeches, and tall black boots that Christina had outgrown last year.

"I do look good," Melanie echoed in amazement. She stood in front of the mirror in Christina's room, staring at her reflection. "Good, but boring."

Christina had to agree. Dressage riders wore traditional black. She preferred the brightly colored helmet covers and shirts that she wore cross-country.

"No one will recognize me without my purple chaps and matching hair," Melanie added.

Christina laughed. "We'll put a sign on you that says, 'This *really* is Melanie.'"

Turning away from the mirror, Melanie looked at Christina with a worried frown. "Do you think Trib is ready for this? He's been so good all week, I keep waiting for him to dump me."

"Hey, you two really hit it off. *You* don't have anything to worry about. *I'm* the one who's going to blow the show," Christina sighed.

"No, you won't. Besides, even if you do, so what? You've decided that you don't want any other horse except Sterling and that's the important thing. If eventing doesn't work out, you two can go into something daring like bareback trick riding. I can see you now—Sterling galloping wildly while you hang from her tail."

Christina laughed at the idea. As she sat on the bed to pull on her boots, her gaze fell on the cover of her eventing magazine. A woman was jumping a horse over a huge stack of logs.

She felt a pang of sadness. *Would that ever be her?* The fact that Sterling had willingly stepped in the water gave Christina renewed hope. But it didn't mean Sterling would ever get used to dressage.

Still, Melanie was right. No matter what happened, Sterling was the horse she wanted, even if it meant never competing in combined training.

Grabbing her helmet, Christina followed Melanie downstairs. The girls had groomed and tacked up the horses earlier, then come inside to change. It was only eight by the time they left the house, but already it was hot. Christina hoped that Mona would relax the dress code and allow them to take off their hunt coats.

Half an hour later, they were riding down the hill toward Gardener Farm. People and horses milled outside the barn. Christina tried to count them, but stopped at twenty riders. Did Mona have that many students?

At the far end of the outdoor ring, a striped canopy was stretched over a picnic table, shading it. That's where Frieda Bruder, the judge, would sit. Christina knew she'd better show Sterling the canopy before they entered the ring.

"Hey, Melanie. Hi, Christina," Cassidy greeted them as they rode up to the barn. She stood next to Foster, who was already tacked up. His mane was braided and his hooves polished. Cassidy had decided to ride Mona's horse since none of hers had ever ridden a dressage test before. Actually, Christina was surprised that Cassidy was even competing today. Ever since her horses had arrived, she'd been busy schooling them in preparation for an upcoming hunter and jumper show in Lexington.

"Hi, Cass," Melanie said cheerily. "How come you don't look wilted like the rest of us?"

Cassidy grinned. She hadn't put on her helmet yet, and her sleek blond hair looked stunning with her black hunt coat. "I guess I'm just naturally coooool," she joked.

"How's the show going?" Christina asked.

"About four of the kids have already ridden their tests," Cassidy told them. The show had started at eight-thirty, but since Melanie and Christina were the only two who had to ride over, Mona had given them later ride times. "Ride times are tacked on the jump standard." Cassidy pointed to a white piece of paper fluttering on the upright standard. "We're using the side pasture for a warm-up area."

"When do you ride?" Melanie asked.

"In fifteen minutes."

"Good luck." Christina steered Sterling over to the standard. Bending down, she read off the names and the times. Melanie rode in thirty minutes. She rode right after that.

Under her helmet, Christina's scalp prickled, and not just from the heat. She was so nervous, her palms were slippery with sweat. She should have brought gloves.

"I can't believe I ride in thirty minutes," Melanie moaned. "I'm never going to remember the test."

"You will, too," Christina assured her cousin. "You were reciting it in your sleep last night."

Melanie closed her eyes and muttered, "Trot to *C*, canter to *K* . . . no, *A* . . . no, *K!*" She slapped her helmet. "See, I've forgotten it already."

"Let's go to the warm-up area and I'll help you practice." Christina pulled a copy of the test from the front pocket of her coat.

"Thanks. But what about you and Sterling?"

"The ride over was our warm-up. Sterling's calm now. Riding her with other horses might get her all jittery."

The two girls rode over to the side pasture. Christina halted Sterling outside the fence while Melanie took Trib inside. Cassidy was trotting Foster in small circles. The pair looked fantastic.

Christina hunted for Dylan and Katie. Two kids about eight years old were also in the pasture, but Christina didn't see her friends. Since Dylan and Katie's ride times were later, Christina assumed they were still in the barn grooming Dakota and Seabreeze.

Turning her attention back to Melanie, Christina noticed that Trib was charging around the pasture, a sour expression on his pony face. And no wonder. Melanie was hanging on the reins and posting stiffly.

"Relax, Mel," Christina called. "Take deep breaths and lighten your grip on the reins. Then slow him with small circles and half halts."

"Right. Right." Melanie bobbed her head. She followed Christina's advice, and in a few minutes Trib's trot had slowed and his ears were pricked.

Christina smiled. *Hey, maybe I know more about this dressage stuff than I thought.* Now, if only she could follow her own advice.

As Cassidy left the ring, Christina wished her good luck again. Then she checked the watch she'd borrowed from her mother. Only half an hour until she had to ride.

Twenty minutes later, Christina and Sterling stood outside the main arena watching Melanie and Trib

151

finish their test. Earlier, Kevin had arrived with Christina's parents. After saying hi to everyone, they'd set lawn chairs under a tree on the other side of the ring and sat down to watch.

Christina was amazed at the number of spectators. People had brought blankets to sit on and beach umbrellas to sit under. Cars were parked in the cross-country field, and kids, horses, and grown-ups swarmed everywhere.

When Melanie trotted Trib into the center of the arena for the final salute, Christina cheered her cousin's performance. She could hardly believe Melanie had done such a great job after only two weeks of lessons. Then with a jolt, she realized it was *her* turn.

Picking up the reins, Christina steered Sterling into the outdoor ring. The judge blew a whistle. Christina had sixty seconds to enter the dressage arena.

Butterflies filled her stomach as she trotted Sterling around the outside perimeter of the arena. As Melanie left the ring, she gave Christina the thumbs-up sign.

We can do this. We can do this, Christina chanted to herself. They were rounding the first corner when a gust of wind hit the judge's tent and it flapped noisily. Sterling leaped sideways, narrowly missing the C marker.

"Easy, girl," Christina soothed. Using lots of leg, she managed to get Sterling past the tent. Quickly, they trotted down the other side and into the dressage arena before the sixty seconds were up.

They trotted to X and halted. Christina took the rein in her left hand, let her right arm drop by her side, and nodded her head in a salute. Sterling pawed, fidgeted, and swung her hips sideways.

Not a great start, Christina thought worriedly.

And it didn't get any better. As they strode off toward C, someone behind the judge's tent slammed a car door shut. Sterling skidded to a stop and eyed the canopy as if waiting for it to attack again.

Christina bit her lip, trying to hold back her frustration. She knew that getting upset wasn't going to calm Sterling, but she couldn't help it. She felt as if all her dreams depended on this one routine. If she and Sterling couldn't get through this, she would have to admit that they'd never make a great eventing team.

Christina didn't know if she had the courage to face that possibility.

Sterling's sitting trot was bone-jarring, and when Christina asked for a canter the mare ducked her head and tried to buck. Her face flushed with embarrassment, Christina sat deep in the saddle, pulled up Sterling's head, and got her moving forward into the turn. But by this time, Sterling was so stretched out that the twenty-meter circle ended up encompassing more than half the ring.

Christina wanted to die. Her mother, her father,

the judge, Mona, Dylan—everybody had to be wincing at her lousy performance.

But that wasn't the worst thing. The worst thing was the way Sterling was fighting her. If dressage meant working in harmony with your horse, then she and Sterling were totally out-of-tune.

You have to relax! she ordered herself.

As they changed rein, Christina inhaled deeply. Focusing on her tense muscles, she willed them to relax. She pretended she and Sterling were alone in one of the pastures and gradually she felt the tension flow from her legs, elbows, and fingers.

Sterling slowed her trot just enough so that Christina could sit without bouncing. *We're halfway through,* she thought. *We're going to make it.*

Suddenly a child's shrill cry rang across the arena.

Startled, Christina almost forgot the next movement. *Canter at* H! Putting her leg back, she asked Sterling for a canter. The mare leaped in the air as if she were coming out of a starting gate on a racetrack. Christina fell forward onto the pommel.

To her surprise, Christina felt Sterling tremble beneath her. Christina remembered how awful she'd felt when she realized Sterling was afraid of water. And now the poor mare was afraid of *everything*—the flapping tent, the loud noises, and the strange new way Christina was asking her to move.

It must be overwhelming for a horse to leave the racetrack, get used to a new rider, and learn a whole new set of commands, Christina realized. *Poor Sterling feels nervous and uncertain. And I've been making it worse. I've been pushing her so hard that she doesn't even know if she can trust me!*

Christina knew that she'd been nervous all morning. And Sterling could sense the tension coming from her rider. The poor horse was terrified, and Christina was making it worse. All of a sudden, the dressage show didn't matter at all. And Christina's dreams of eventing didn't matter. All that mattered was Sterling. Christina had to comfort the horse she loved. She had to make Sterling feel safe and calm.

I've got to show her it's okay if she doesn't know exactly how to do dressage yet, Christina thought. She relaxed her seat bones in the saddle, trying to balance Sterling and bend her into the turn. As they cantered across the arena, she didn't think about the judge. She just concentrated on her mare.

Christina took a deep breath and let the tension drain out of her body. Sterling's hooves pounded with the beating of her own heart. Christina's body swayed with every movement her horse made.

"That's right, girl," she whispered. "Just calm down and remember how much we love riding together."

Slowly, she felt Sterling's jarring canter become softer, smoother. Then Sterling dropped her nose and rounded her back—just like a real dressage horse.

Sitting deep, Christina asked Sterling for the final trot. Instantly, the mare made the transition as if she'd read Christina's mind. Keeping light contact on the reins, she let Sterling stretch out. Her stride was so long and graceful, Christina felt as if they were floating.

It was so wonderful, she wanted to cry.

Trotting into the center, Christina asked for the halt. Without hesitation or resistance, Sterling stopped square and stood quietly. Clapping rang across the arena, but Christina was oblivious. She knew her score would be low, but it didn't matter. For a few magical moments, she and Sterling had been working in total harmony.

Now Christina knew for sure that Sterling was—and always would be—her dream horse.

"Watch out, Christina!" Melanie shouted.

Christina spun around, her Super Soaker ready, but she was too late. Dylan blasted her. "Gotcha!"

Shielding her face with one hand, Christina raced around the corner of the house. She ducked behind a bush and crouched down. She waited, listening to the happy screeches coming from the front yard.

Dylan was right—after a hard day, getting together with friends was important. And so far, the party was a huge success. They'd gobbled the burgers, hot dogs, and salads. Then they'd divided into two teams—girls against the guys—and the water battle had begun. Everybody had been eager to cool down and blow off some steam.

Christina tensed as she heard the muffled thud of bare feet on grass. Moving stealthily, Dylan crept around the corner. He looked right, then left, and when he didn't see anyone, he began to run across the backyard.

Jumping up, Christina gave a war whoop, aimed, and pulled the trigger. The full force of her Super Soaker shot Dylan in the chest. With a growl of mock anger, he lunged for her. She turned to run, but he tackled her around the legs and they both tumbled to the grass.

"I got you good that time!" Christina crowed.

"Oh, really? I'm not as wet as you are."

Christina glanced down at the cutoffs she'd worn over her tank-style bathing suit. They were soaked, and her hair hung in wet noodles. "You're right." She laughed, but when she realized Dylan was lying across her legs she blushed and scrambled to a sitting position. Just as quickly, he sat up and nervously ran his fingers through his damp hair.

"This is just what we needed after the hot show," he said. "I'm glad you decided to do it."

"Even if I did get the worst score of the day?"

Dylan ducked his chin, but couldn't hide his grin. "It was pretty bad. But hey, you took it like a pro."

"That's because winning wasn't important. Finding out that Sterling and I were working together as partners was all that mattered."

"So what did Frieda the Judge say to you when she went over your scores?"

Christina made her voice low: "Dat vas an interesting test!" she recited in a German accent.

Dylan threw back his head and laughed.

"Well, what did she say about *yours*?"

"Not telling."

"Go on. I know you did great."

"She said that Dakota and I had potential and that she had some ideas she'd share with me at her clinic next week."

"So you're definitely going?"

"Yup."

"Great!" Christina beamed. "Of course she insisted that I come to her clinic. She said, 'Ve haf much vork to do!' She even intimidated my mother into giving me permission to go!"

They both laughed again. Christina heard Melanie hollering from the front yard for everyone to come and get cake. But she and Dylan didn't move.

Side by side, they sat silently in the grass. The sun was setting and a warm breeze began to blow. Christina thought this was a perfect ending to the day.

Almost the ending, she corrected herself. Later, she wanted to tell her mother that her advice had been absolutely right. Relationships that were important did take time—both with boys *and* horses.

Christina smiled, thinking of Sterling. With a little

patience, she had managed to rebuild the trust between herself and the mare. Now she was certain Sterling was the right horse for her. Even though their score was bad, this show had been an amazing experience.

And Christina had a feeling their next show would be even better!

Will Christina make a new friend at Camp
Saddlebrook—or a new enemy?
Find out in *Thoroughbred* #28,
Camp Saddlebrook, coming in July 1998.
Here's a preview:

"YOU ARE *SO* BAD," CHRISTINA SCOLDED STERLING. "IF YOU
had to chew, why didn't you pick something inexpen-
sive, like a lead line?"

Even though the neatsfoot oil Christina rubbed into
the chewed leather helped erase the worst of the
scratches, Sterling's teeth had left the rein bumpy and
bent in two places. It wasn't damaged to the point that
it might break, but the rein still looked chewed.

Christina draped the bridle over her arm and stood.
"I guess I'll have to break the news to Eliza."

Eliza was lying on her stomach reading when
Christina walked into the cabin.

"I'm really sorry," Christina began, her thumb and
finger still trying to smooth out the holes in the rein.
"But Sterling got hold of Flash's bridle."

Eliza wiggled to a sitting position and held out her

hand. When she saw the chew marks, her mouth tight-ened.

"It's not really cut or anything," Christina stam-mered. "I put some oil on it and that made it look a lot better. I bet after it's used and cleaned a few times, it will stretch right out again."

Eliza closed her fist around the rein. "You should have told me Sterling chewed. I would have hung it on the other side." She stared at her hand while she spoke.

"I didn't know she did," Christina said. "At home we keep our stuff in a tack room."

Eliza rolled her eyes. "Well, I guess we don't have the setup you have at home. If your horse is the type that grabs things, you're supposed to bring a stall guard to keep her head in."

She doesn't have to be so nasty, Christina thought. If Eliza had put the bridle away in her tack trunk instead of letting it hang outside, Sterling wouldn't have been able to get at it in the first place.

"I don't want to have to keep the bridle in my trunk," Eliza continued as if she'd read Christina's mind. "There's not enough room, and the leather gets musty if it doesn't have air."

"I'll go to the tack shop down the road and buy a stall guard tomorrow," Christina said. "My parents opened an account for me in case of an emergency." She laughed a little, trying to lighten things up. "And I guess *this* is an emergency."

Eliza stared at Christina for a moment, a frown curling her lips. Then she grunted and hung the bridle on the corner of the bed. She stretched out again and rolled over.

Christina sighed. Clearly, Eliza wasn't going to talk to her for the rest of the night.

I thought camp was supposed to be fun, she thought. *But it's no fun getting the silent treatment from your cabinmate. What is Eliza's problem, anyway?*

It was just her luck that she'd been stuck rooming with the one girl at camp who didn't seem to like her. And on top of that, their horses were stabled right next to each other.

Sterling and Flash obviously don't get along very well, either, Christina thought.

Somehow, she had a feeling that things were going to get even worse before camp was over . . .

Eliza stepped out of Flash's stall. Even in the dim light, Christina could tell her eyes were puffy and red.

"I bet he'll be fine," Christina said. "We've had a lot of horses colic, maybe even fifty, and there's only one that died."

"Really?" Eliza's voice was small.

"Oh, yeah," Christina said, trying to sound like it was something that happened every day. "A lot of horses do it when they travel to a new place. And people are always shipping us mares for breeding." She

163

paused. "I wonder if that's why he colicked? Maybe he didn't drink enough water or something because it smelled strange to him. I know Sterling sometimes won't drink the water when we go to a show." Christina knew she was babbling, but Eliza didn't seem to mind.

Eliza wiped her nose on the sleeve of her T-shirt. "I don't think it was the hay or grain. I'm always really careful to smell them to make sure they aren't moldy before I feed them." She sniffed again. "You don't have any tissues, do you?"

"No," Christina said. "But how about some paper towels? I always keep a roll in my trunk." She found a sheet and passed it to Eliza.

"Thanks."

Christina tactfully left Eliza to mop her face and blow her nose in private. She grabbed her tack bucket, ran some water into it, and started to work on Trib's bit.

Eliza shoved the paper towel in her pocket and leaned against the stall door. "I haven't thanked you for what you did."

"It was nothing."

"You probably saved Flash's life. If he had died, I don't know what I would have done."

"Don't think about that," Christina said, noticing that Eliza's eyes were filling with tears again.

"I have to," she said through clenched teeth. "He doesn't even belong to me."

Christina stopped rubbing the bit. "What?"

"He's not mine. A woman at my barn is trying to sell him because he's too hard for her to handle. My instructor talked her into letting me bring him to camp so he could have more experience. And because she knew I needed a horse to ride." The words spilled out like they had been bottled up inside and someone had opened the cork.

"But you've been coming to Saddlebrook for years," Christina protested. "You must have a horse." Besides, Eliza didn't ride like someone who only rode once a week at a lesson.

"I do, but he's too old for this much work now. My instructor uses him to give lessons to beginners."

"Why don't you buy Flash then? You guys are perfect for each other."

Eliza looked down at her feet. "I've been baby-sitting and saving up all winter, but I don't have nearly enough."

"Won't your parents help?"

"They were going to, but then someone bought the company my dad worked for, and they downsized."

"You mean he got fired?" Christina gasped.

"No," Eliza said, her voice rising. "It wasn't his fault he got laid off." Her eyes narrowed as she glared at Christina. "You rich kids don't know anything."

Christina felt like she'd been slapped in the face. "I'm not rich."

"Well, what do *you* call it, then? You have your own Thoroughbred and practically a whole tack shop in that custom made trunk of yours. To say nothing of a groom that delivers it for you."

"Look," Christina said, throwing the sponge she was using into the bucket. "It's not my fault my parents are in the horse business. I'd much rather have had them drive me to camp instead of someone who works for them, but they were too busy. And sure, I've got a lot of tack and stuff, but most of it is things my parents don't use anymore."

"Oh, forget it," Eliza said, turning to go back into Flash's stall.

"No." Christina stood up, wincing as her scraped skin resisted stretching. "You've been snotty to me ever since I came, and I haven't done anything to you. And for your information, the reason my tack trunk is so big is because my father built it for me and it turned out bigger than he thought it would be. But I guess that makes it custom made." Christina took a few steps away, then turned back.

"And I know I'm lucky to have Sterling, but don't make me out to be a stuck-up rich kid. I work hard around our farm, and so do my parents. I'm sorry that you don't have a horse right now and I'm sorry your father lost his job. But if anyone is acting stuck-up around here, it's you!"

She emptied the dirty water and stuffed Trib's bridle into Melanie's trunk.

That's it, she thought angrily. *Eliza and I are officially at war!*

ALICE LEONHARDT has been horse crazy since she was five years old. Her first pony was a pinto named Ted. When she got older, she joined Pony Club and rode in shows and rallies. Now she just rides her quarter horse, April, for fun. The author of over thirty books for children, she still finds time to take care of two horses, two cats, two dogs, and two children, as well as teach at a community college.